The more I
LEARNED,
the less I
KNEW

The more I
LEARNED,
the less I
KNEW

A teacher's memories

ERNIE GABRIELSON

iUniverse, Inc.
Bloomington

The more I learned, the less I knew
A teacher's memories

iUniverse books may be ordered through booksellers or by contacting:

iUniverse
1663 Liberty Drive
Bloomington, IN 47403
www.iuniverse.com
1-800-Authors (1-800-288-4677)

ISBN: 978-1-4759-5461-6 (sc)
ISBN: 978-1-4759-5462-3 (ebk)

Printed in the United States of America

iUniverse rev. date: 10/19/2012

THIS BOOK IS RESPECTFULLY DEDICATED TO
ALL THE TEACHERS EVERYWHERE WHO STRIVE
EVERY DAY IN EVERY WAY TO OPEN THE
MINDS OF THEIR STUDENTS.

Acknowledgement

This book could not have been written without the help of Jacque Wallace who did the editing and helped in other ways—too many to mention.

The end-of-chapter quotations come from two great books. *Wise Words and Quotes* by Vern McLellan and *The Quotable Teacher* edited by Randy Howe

Preface

Like everyone else, I've made some bad decisions in my life, but deciding to become a teacher was never one of them. When I was released from the Marine Corps to reserve status after serving in Korea; the officer who signed my papers indicated since the Corps needed experienced men, I would receive a large bonus, an additional stripe and my choice of duty stations if I would ship over. He was critical of my decision to enroll in college to become a teacher. "Sergeant, you'll never make as much money teaching as you will in the Corps."

But in spite of this huge temptation, I enrolled in college and began studying for a future career in teaching. Friends who earned much more money than I ever did often told me I could have done much better—at least financially. My family had to struggle at times because I didn't make much as a teacher, but I stayed with it since I believe education is very important; and more to the point, I loved my job.

Years after retirement, I look back on my teaching career with joy. I don't think I ever had a boring day in over 30 years. I met many idealistic, dedicated teachers I number among my friends still today. Also, many of my former students have told me I made a difference in their lives. That, alone, made it impossible to believe I would ever have been happy doing something else, even though the financial rewards might have been greater.

After I retired from Mingus Union High in Cottonwood, Arizona, I didn't really quit teaching. I became an adjunct faculty member at our local community college. I also had opportunities to consult with a few inexperienced teachers as well and offered to share things I had learned about teaching.

All teachers know none of us ever become an "expert" in our field because every day teachers learn something new.

After my wife, Carroll, died in 2005, I helped a teacher by working with some of her students who needed to pass the AIMS writing test in order to graduate. I'm proud to say they all passed. Diminished eyesight forced me to quit driving, and I decided to come to Tucson and to take advantage of its excellent bus service as well as to be close to my son and grandson. I began living in a wonderful retirement complex where I continue to be active and happy.

In 2007, my teaching career entered a new phase. One day I was in line at a book store waiting to pay for a book. I looked behind me and began talking with a small boy who was carrying about five books. He was accompanied by his mother and grandmother. Since it was the beginning of summer vacation, I asked him what grade he was in. He replied, "I just graduated from the first grade, Sir."

I knew the books he held were on at least the fifth grade level, so I asked, "Are those books for you?"

"Yes," he replied. "I've read all the rest of the series. I love reading, and I read everything I can."

Against his mother's protest, I grabbed his books, "I'm going to pay for your books because I'm very proud of you."

I told Laura Perkins, who was with me, buying his books gave me a very warm, good feeling.

She wisely replied, "Then, Ernie, why don't you do it more often?"

Thus began my new career—giving books to kids. I began to buy many books to hand out to kids at malls, buses, or ball games, etc. Like Johnnie Appleseed, who traveled throughout the United States spreading seeds to grow apple trees, I wanted to spark as many kids into reading as I could.

One of my old lessons as an active teacher was *to give the right book to the right kid at the right time.* I later was invited to classrooms to give books out after giving a short talk about the value of reading. I guess I'll never really retire from teaching, and I never want to. Like Geoffrey Chaucer's Oxford Scholar in the *Canterbury Tales*, "Gladly would I learn and gladly teach."

Chapter 1

I was very nervous as I stood outside the auditorium at Chandler High School while waiting for my very first faculty meeting. Almost trembling with fright, I wished for a cigarette but saw no one smoking, so I didn't dare light up. Two weeks before this warm September day, I had signed my first teaching contract, but on this day, I wished I hadn't. I was dressed as formally as I could—even wearing a necktie. Several others were dressed as I was, and I guessed they were also new to the system. Others, however, were dressed very casually and were standing around laughing and joking with friends. These were, of course, the veteran teachers. At some sort of signal, we all started filing into the large auditorium. A person at the door directed each of us to the school section to which we were assigned. I was directed to the junior high section.

As I took a seat, several of the veterans introduced themselves and shook my hand. I responded very stiffly because their friendliness didn't completely rid me of my jitters. Before the speeches began, I thought of several times I had faced a new adventure and had overcome my fears. I thought of my first day underground in the mine in Bisbee when a cage zoomed me and many others down 2000 feet below the surface.

Then I thought of the time my training battalion was formed up to hear a general bid us farewell as we left Camp Pendleton and the United States. Under full packs, we stood before the speaker's platform. Among other things the general said, "I envy you young men. You are going to Korea and to the biggest adventure of your lives. I regret some of you won't return, but those who do will never forget the experience." I don't believe my year of serving in a Marine line company gave me fear that equaled my fears on that September morning. I wondered *what am I doing here in a room loaded with experienced professionals? I don't belong here.*

The superintendent of all the schools in Chandler welcomed us, and then each of the principals gave an inspirational talk.

At about noon, we were dismissed for lunch. After lunch, we were to use the afternoon to prepare our classrooms to welcome the students three days later. The highlight of the day was having three of the veteran teachers invite me to have lunch with them at a nearby restaurant. As we talked over lunch, they did their best to ease my fears. They all confessed they also had experienced the same feelings I was facing when they started their careers.

When we returned to school and to our empty and silent classrooms, I started putting things in order. Both of my neighbors came in, introduced themselves, and offered to help me arrange books, etc. Mr. Simmons and Mrs. Deaver, who were both veteran teachers with more than 20 years of service, said if I should run into trouble, I could seek help from them.

Three days later, I stood by the teacher's desk waiting for the onrush of students as they came in for their first day of school. Then, I believe, my fear was greater than on the first meeting with the teachers and principals. Coming in, many continued with conversations with friends while others looked me over. I shakily wrote my name on the chalkboard and introduced myself. I had each of my class of 8-1 English students introduce themselves. Then I began the process of issuing them three books—one for spelling, one for reading, and one for grammar and language. It was then I found those youngsters were all sort of "pulling for me." This was to be my homeroom class which would return later in the morning for a 20-minute "activity" period. They were with me for a two-hour block of time to study Language Arts.

After they left, I had two other groups come in for their two-hour sessions. When the final bell rang at 3:30, I was a little surprised I had survived a test and was more relaxed as I left the school grounds in my new Dodge.

Although I had first-day school jitters for 32 years, I always look back to the very first one in 1955 and smile. As my experience grew through the years, I did my best to take our incoming, "new" teachers to lunch hoping to reduce the same fears I had faced. Several veterans always came along to help. I don't believe I will ever get over the joy I had when welcoming new classes of students.

I taught at Chandler Junior High for three years and learned many things. Anna, the teacher in <u>The King and I</u>, a Broadway musical, sings of learning more from her students than she ever taught them. That certainly is true in my case.

Retirement is wonderful in its way, but one never gets over the excitement of the first day of school. Like the general said, "I envy those as they start the unforgettable experience of teaching." I hope this little book might help some new teachers as I learned some "tricks of the trade" from my colleagues and students every day as I entered a classroom.

> "My first year has been disappointing as it was rewarding . . . I have lost and found hope, reviewed and revised, and finally concluded that my presence here is much more important than I had thought it would be,"
> Catherine McTamaney.

Chapter 2

I learned a lot in my three years at Chandler Junior High. I think the biggest thing the beginning teacher has to learn is he is standing in front of 25 or so individuals—not just a class. Unlike college classrooms, one size doesn't fit all. I soon discovered education is a path made of many steps. Some of the students are well ahead on the path, while others lag behind. Many of the teachers we had in college merely taught from yellowed notes or lectured to the class from a prepared lesson plan developed to teach a subject. Of course, lesson plans are necessary, but the conscientious teacher in elementary or high school needs to do his level best to bring the students who are lagging behind up a few steps while not boring those who are well along on the path. Good teachers teach students as well as subjects.

In my experience as teacher and principal, I observed many teachers who were too lazy to recognize individuals. One of the best things one can see as a teacher is a little light in a poor student's eyes as the material sinks in. In my early days of teaching, I mistakenly called often on the brightest kids to respond to questions because I was relatively sure to get the right answer. It is a truism that often those responses rub off on the poor student (sort of a trickle-down effect), but often those responses don't. I learned early asking questions was a much better educational tool than simply lecturing to the whole class about the material. When a poor student gets an answer right, the answer is a step on the path of learning. It is a bigger step for him than it is for the students who are the brightest.

During the activity period, instead of having students work on assignments alone from math, science or history; I would wander around and try to help the poor students get the right answers on their homework. I seldom had to do this with my 8-1 class because they were more homogeneously grouped since they were all band students. I began to like teaching the 8-3s or 8-6s more because there was a wider variety of academic talent in the class when it came to being on the learning path.

Sure, I felt good about standing in front of the 8-1s because I falsely felt their good grades were wholly a result of my good teaching. The falsity of this thinking was brought home to me graphically one day when a student asked if a comma was always necessary in a compound sentence. I responded that short sentences did not need a comma. Almost immediately there was a gasp of disbelief from a few in the class. Some turned to pages in their notebooks from the seventh grade, checking on whether I was right. Later during the activity period, Mrs. Grey, a very experienced teacher, came to my door and asked to see me outside. I was nervous about this because some of the 8-1s had previously told me Mrs. Grey had given them many "rules" and made them keep those rules in a notebook while they were in her class.

"What do you mean, Mr. Gabrielson, telling students they don't need a comma in a compound sentence?"

Finding I had violated a "sacred rule of grammar," I stammered nervously, "I told them a comma wasn't always necessary if the sentence was very short. I said perhaps a sentence like *Jack fell and Jill cried* wouldn't necessarily need a comma."

Mrs. Grey stormed away saying something about recent college graduates. I guess I won the battle that time, but Mrs. Grey won the war big time. She had over 25 years experience on me, and I often went to her seeking advice. She and I became fast friends. I encourage all beginning teachers to hop on the "experience train" and learn from all the teachers around them even though they might appear to be a little old fashioned. Mrs. Grey had a wonderful sense of humor, and she taught me to use mine in the classroom. This is a weapon I used in my entire teaching career; and it's, perhaps, the best weapon in a teacher's arsenal.

That year my 8-1 home room won nearly everything—academic and athletic. There was a magazine selling drive with a television set as the grand prize. Rae Lou Appleby, a wonderful young lady, won this in spite of the competition of the principal's daughter in another grade. Since we won every time out, I thought I was a pretty fair teacher. Then I had to change my mind.

The next year, the principal assigned me the 8-6s as my homeroom. These were students who were behind all their classmates in almost everything. The 8-6s were students who came to my class unable to cope with most of the lessons I was trying to teach. However, I think I learned more about teaching from them than I did from the 8-1s. They all took developmental reading from Mrs. Deaver, my neighbor next door. She was the most experienced teacher at our school. In addition, she was very nice and charming. Patience was her strong point. Her classes had a wide range of reading abilities, ranging from the first grade to about the fifth grade level.

One day, during the activity period, I went back and started conversation with a very nice boy named LB. Several students gathered around when I asked LB to learn something to ask Mrs. Deaver. I had him write, "Education is the acquisition of the art of the utilization of knowledge." After explaining what this meant to LB and others in plainer language, I had him memorize it. Then I asked him to raise his hand in Mrs. Deaver's class and ask her if it were true. Many of the kids got hopped up and helped LB's effort to memorize it. During the next hour, I heard an explosion of laughter coming from the reading classroom. In about five minutes, Mrs. Deaver came to my door, smiling and saying she almost fainted when LB came out with A.N. Whitehead's definition of education.

The next day, LB was something of a class hero in the activity period, and several of the other students asked, "Give me one, Mr. Gabrielson. I want to see Mrs. Deaver's face when I say it." I gave them lines of poetry and just about wore out Bartlett's quotation book. I found they were proud to have learned something "outside" of their textbooks. As we all laughed, I found them a bit more eager to learn. The lesson? Humor works wonders. This trick was one I used extensively in each of my teaching years.

I did the little trick with LB just to give some of our students a little laugh. However, when many students wanted a famous saying to spring on their teachers, I could see they were excited about learning even if it were only a sentence or two.

When I thought about it later, an idea came to me. If the students were a bit inspired by LB's speech, the excitement might carry over to regular lessons. It was then I started giving extra credit for students doing something which might inspire learning in others. I used versions of letting students show others learning is both fun and exciting.

One of the best examples of this and one of my happiest times as a teacher occurred many years later when I was teaching the Arthurian legend at Mingus Union. An <u>A</u> student came up to my desk after class and asked, "Can I do something for extra credit?"

I assured her she didn't need to do anything extra as she certainly would receive an <u>A</u>.

"But I want to be sure, Mr. Gabrielson. I have time and I like what we're studying."

She was not only an honor student in academic classes, but she participated in sports and drama. She had been the lead in all the student plays for the past two years. The girl was good—very good in everything she tried.

While writing this, I've been told her name is Nancy Ware. I confess I had forgotten her name.

I gave her my copy of Tennyson's *Idylls of the King*. Near the end of Book 11, there is a scene when Arthur comes to visit Guinevere at the Nunnery. He comes to bid her goodbye and to forgive her for her sin. She realizes he loved her very much, and she should have loved him instead of sinning with Lancelot. When he leaves, she rushes to the window to see him mounting his horse to go to his last battle. At this point in the poem, she has a very long monologue while thinking of how wonderful he and the Round Table were.

I asked, "I know you've studied Reader's Theater. Can you read this monologue aloud in class putting some drama into it?" The monologue covered about six pages of material.

She smiled and took the book. "I'll try to do a good job with it."

I knew she was working on it during the next couple of days. Then I asked her if she was ready. "No, Sir. I'll be ready when I stop crying when I read it."

Over a week passed before she said she was ready. I told the class about the situation and then turned the class over to her. I was totally surprised to note she didn't use the book, but had memorized the whole thing. I wasn't surprised, however, when I saw the entire class was paying strict attention to her. I even noted she had some of them crying—including some big, tough, football players. It was magnificent! I believe no actress in Hollywood could have done better. Before I could offer my congratulations about her wonderful job, the classroom erupted in applause. I knew even the most reluctant students would like the lessons on King Arthur better because of hearing her performance.

As I offered my congratulations and thanks, she asked with a smile, "Do I get extra credit for that?"

"No, you don't. Not until you come to my fourth period class and do it again." I enjoyed the puzzled look on her face for a moment before she smiled, "You'll have to write a note to my fourth period teacher so I can come."

I gave her the note and she came. If anything, the second performance was better than the first. The students were enraptured and broke into applause. "Now do I get the extra credit?"

"Not until you do this for the fifth period." I don't think she was surprised by this and was probably a bit flattered by my request.

During the lunch hour, I went to the office of the highest administrator and asked him to come to my class next period. Mr. Barber shuffled some papers as he told me he had too much to do. It was the standard administrator cop out. I said, "Mr. Barber, I sincerely want you to come. My whole class wants you to come. We are doing something you don't want to miss and probably will never forget. My students would love it if you'd be there. You can use the period to evaluate me if you wish."

While I was setting the scene before her performance, Mr. Barber came in. He stood at the door so he could leave early if he desired. The young lady again enraptured the whole class—including the superintendent. Again she had many students wiping away tears. When the applause died, I went up to her. She didn't have to ask about extra credit. "You have earned so much extra credit today if you sleep in my class the rest of the year, you'll still get an A."

Mr. Barber came up next and congratulated her. "That's one of the best things I've ever heard a student do."

Of course, she didn't sleep and worked as hard as ever. During the next year after she went to college, she came into my classroom one day. "Mr. Gabrielson, guess what? I have the lead in the play we're doing at the university. I tried out for the part by auditioning with the same thing I did in your classes last year."

I really couldn't help it, but I hugged her and said, "I know you made a few believers last year. Thank you for one of the best memories I've had in all my years of teaching."

I guess the lesson here is to let students take over when you can. Sometimes they inspire those who you might otherwise have difficulty inspiring.

> "Only the curious will learn and only the resolute overcome the obstacles to learning. The quest quotient has always excited me more than the intelligence quotient,"
> Eugene S. Wilson

Chapter 3

My third year teaching in the junior high began pretty much as the previous ones. I was assigned the 8-6s again as my homeroom class. That year would bring a lot of changes—both in teaching and my personal life. A tall math teacher, Tom McGaffic, and I became good friends. Tom had played center in basketball for Slippery Rock College. He was about 6'6" in height. I guess we became friends because we were the only unmarried men on the faculty. He and I would go into Phoenix every weekend, hoping to enjoy some female companionship, but we nearly always failed.

One day, he and I were talking in the crowded faculty room in the midst of several other conversations. I mentioned our school should have a yearbook. He agreed, and I thought that was the end of it. However, Mr. Knox, the principal, called me in after school and asked if I would be the sponsor of a yearbook. I guessed someone had told him I mentioned it earlier.

So began another new adventure. The students were all for having a yearbook but never dreamed what a headache its production would give me. I went to a publisher's representative in Phoenix and received a lot of materials and advice. He had been a college classmate of mine, so I enlisted him and his company to publish it.

Every afternoon several students came in and helped cut and paste class pictures onto specially marked blank pages. We scheduled picture taking for all our teams as well as several other activities. Needless to say, I learned a lot about yearbook production. After driving to Phoenix many times with the pages in a battered red box, we felt it was completed. Tom helped considerably by designing the cover. As the book neared completion, we asked the student body to suggest a name. Overwhelmingly, the name selected was *Panther Cry*. The book was a resounding success, and by cutting corners, it paid for itself. Even Mr. Knox, who wasn't often given to praise my efforts, was pleased. It was Chandler Junior High's first yearbook. It proved if kids want a thing badly enough, they'll work hard to achieve it even if they have to stay after school.

While working overtime on the book, my personal life underwent a dramatic change. My brother married a nurse from Good Samaritan Hospital in the fall. When Tom and I went to my folks' house in Phoenix, we occasionally met Charlie and his new bride there. We teased him a bit which bothered Carolyn, his bride. One day she told us she was arranging for us to meet two classmates of hers. We went on a blind date, and that's how I met Carroll, the girl I fell in love with and married.

Carroll and I, like most newlyweds, went searching for a house. We looked at the most inexpensive tract homes and finally found one we liked in Phoenix. However, when we were in the process of purchasing, we were told I didn't make enough money for FHA or VA financing. The loan officer said they would not include Carroll's salary because she *might* get pregnant and have to quit her job. (That was the mortgage loan policy before women's lib.)

When I discovered after three years of teaching, I still couldn't buy a house, I determined to quit and accept a full-time job with my summer employer. They were wholesale suppliers of candy and tobacco. Even at a poor hourly wage with them, I would make more money than I had as a teacher. Both bosses also promised if I worked full time, they would raise my salary considerably and promote me to sales when an opening came up. That was irresistible. I turned in my tenure contract, and Carroll and I moved to an apartment in Phoenix. We both worked and made a vow to one day buy a house.

Late that summer, Fate took a hand in our lives. I told Carroll regardless of the money, I wanted to go back to teaching but this time in a high school. However, all teachers and prospective teachers know late August is not a good time to be seeking a job in teaching. I went to various Phoenix high schools only to be told they were fully staffed. In the last days of August, the Education Employment Office at Arizona State informed me there was a late posting for an English and journalism teacher at Kingman. The only journalism training I had was in high school, but I was desperate.

I called Mr. Joy, the superintendent of schools, and was immediately hired over the phone. "Don't you want my papers and an interview with me?" I asked.

"It's only a week before school starts, and I need an English and journalism teacher, and you're our man. I'll send for your papers."

When I left Chandler Junior High, I had some regrets. Many of the teaching staff there were my mentors and friends. I remember them fondly because they all helped me as I began my teaching career. I would see Mrs. Grey again at her retirement party several years later. I was happy to receive an invitation to it about 10 years after I left Chandler. Many of her "kids" and fellow teachers came. I hugged and kissed her with tears in my eyes. Young teachers should all have someone like her to help them, and they need to make the effort required to find them.

When I was in the Marine Corps, I read a poem written by a Marine who had been a line trooper at Iwo Jima. I can't remember much of it, but a couple of lines are a good lesson for teachers as well as for Marines.

> *It's the old guys who anchor the line,*
> *When hell comes rolling in.*

I found those lines to be true when I was a line Marine in Korea and again when I began teaching at Chandler.

Not yet having a whole lot to pack, Carroll and I (and the dog) drove to Kingman the night before the first faculty meeting. I had previously rented a house with a yard for the dog. The rent was $40 a month. This was less than half of what we were paying in Phoenix.

I was to spend two years in Kingman before we moved to the Verde Valley, Carroll's beloved home area. Mohave Union High School, in spite of many years of service, looked awfully good to me as I climbed the steps at the entrance for the first time in August 1958.

> "Experienced teachers . . . are an invaluable resource to the [first-year] teachers who are willing to admit that they have much to learn,"
> Robert Gress.

Chapter 4

At the first teacher's meeting in Kingman, I looked around to spot the experienced teachers I hoped would continue my teaching education. When Mr. Joy, the superintendent, spoke, I knew he would be one to give good advice. I was especially impressed by Lee Williams, the principal. During my two years at Kingman, he helped me more than I could ever measure. (Several years after I left Kingman, Lee was killed in a horrible accident. He was a volunteer firefighter and responded when a railroad car caught fire and later exploded, killing several people in addition to Lee.)

Going along with my teaching duties, I was given the responsibility of writing about the activities at school for the *Mohave Miner*, the area newspaper. I was glad I was given that assignment because the owner and editor of the paper was a high school classmate and friend of my older brother. When I talked about this assignment with Dick Waters, he agreed to make me a "stringer." In the old days of news reporting, one would measure the inches in all his stories with a string. This string was measured periodically and the writer was paid by the number of inches. Mr. Waters agreed to pay me ten cents an inch for anything coming from the school, whether I wrote it or not. I know the pay doesn't sound good today, but then it was an excellent supplement to my meager teacher's salary. I learned a lot about writing and journalism because Dick was a wonderful teacher and friend.

Writing articles about all the programs at the school, including sports gave me an opportunity to widen my view of the complete school program and to meet with the teachers who were involved in other programs. Many of these teachers became good friends of mine because of my "reporting."

On the first day of school, I was a bit floored by the size of my students since I was used to junior high kids. I found out the more-mature high schoolers were a little more serious in their studies. My four classes of Junior English and my Journalism class consisted of nice kids who, again, I found "pullin' for me."

Not knowing much about journalism, that class scared me more than the other English classes. We were to put out a paper periodically with a mimeograph machine. I doubt if any of those exist today, but it was common then to have stories typed on wax stencils and then these were attached to the machine. After the machine printed the required number of pages, the stencil was lifted off the machine, and we hoped the ink on it didn't jump onto our clothes and skin. Fortunately I had very good students who really wanted a good paper and worked hard at getting the job done. Another lesson learned: *Trust your students because they want the product to be good, just as the teacher does.*

Inevitably some students didn't measure up on tests and assignments in spite of my best efforts. It's hard to keep all the students "on the ball" all the time. I learned very quickly many students considered romance, athletics, drama, etcetera more important than many of my English lessons as good as I thought they were. As hard as I tried, I found it almost impossible to keep a football player's mind on Shakespeare the day of the big game.

On those days I tried to reach the players using many different tactics. I started classes by talking football and the game for a few minutes. I would usually get them to participate in the discussion which brought their minds back into the English classroom. I tried to do this as subtly as I could. By then, I had learned not to give difficult, important assignments just before the day of the game or a big social event.

One of the best players on our team was a big fellow who was nice and polite, but that semester he focused too much on football and girls and not nearly enough on class work. In spite of my trying to get him involved in the English curriculum, he usually had his mind elsewhere. As a result, he failed the first semester. Sometimes students who fail blame the teacher, but Sam didn't. As I told him he had failed, he smiled and said, "Well, Mr. Gabrielson, you did your best."

I was mildly surprised when he came into my class starting the second semester. He could have gone to Mrs. Logston, another junior English instructor, because he had a choice. As he came into the classroom, I welcomed him with, "Good to see you again, Sam. I hope you'll work harder this semester." He assured me he'd try harder. For a while, he did and then he started slipping into his old habit of not doing the homework. One day when I talked to him about it, he said, "I just don't get some of them authors, and they don't write about stuff that interests me."

It was then I discovered one of the best teaching tricks. I gave him a small book to read called, *Mr. Roberts.* The book was very popular and had become a hit Broadway show as well as a hit movie. It's about sailors on a ship who constantly worked against a stupid and harsh captain. It was set in World War II and had a bit of rough language in it. While he had the book, I worried his parents might see it and wonder why he was reading it instead of his good, safe assignments. About two weeks later, Sam returned the book to me, saying, "Mr. Gabrielson, that was the best book I ever read. Do you have any more like it?" I told him that I'd give him another one if he would promise to work harder on the regular assignments in the text books.

Next he read Hemingway's *A Farewell to Arms*, which he liked. He worked on his regular assignments and passed with a <u>C</u>. The lesson was very simple, but golden: *Give the right book to the right kid at the right time and the spark sometimes ignites into flames.*

That happened to me at Bisbee High years before I began teaching. My sophomore teacher assigned us to read a book of our choice. I forgot to bring a book to class so she suggested I read *The Count of Monte Cristo*. When I went to the library for the book, I learned it was over 1000 pages. I told her I didn't want to read a book that long. She told me if I read 100 pages I would get full credit. What a deal! But she fooled me. After I read the 100 pages, I was unable to put the book down. I know of no one who can read 100 pages of that book and then put it down. Dumas was absolutely fabulous; and I, like Sam, was hooked into a lifetime of reading.

During my first year at Kingman, my lovely wife, Carroll, became pregnant; and in March, my son Mike was born. She wanted to return to her beloved Verde Valley to be near her parents. I told her I'd apply to Mingus High. I talked this over with O.B. Joy, my boss. He advised me to stay in Kingman since Mingus was going through many troubles that year, and, hopefully, those troubles would end by the next year.

We both liked Kingman very much, so staying on an extra year was not a real disappointment to either of us. Carroll liked the neighbors, and I had strong friendships with many of the faculty. At the time, Kingman was a very nice, small town located very near Laughlin and Las Vegas. The famous Highway 66 ran right through it. The main street was named for one of Kingman's best known and beloved persons—the movie star, Andy Devine. He was born and raised there.

> "The art of teaching is the art of assisting discovery,"
> Mark Van Doren (1894-1973).

Chapter 5

In 1959, during the spring of my second year, Mr. Joy called me into his office to tell me Mingus High now had a wonderful man as superintendent, and the problems of the previous year had been eliminated. Carroll was overjoyed with the prospect, but I loved Kingman High and was reluctant to leave a place I loved only to start another adventure at a new school.

Because of Carroll's urging, I went down for an interview with Mingus High's new superintendent, Mr. West, and applied for an English and Journalism job that was open. I mentioned I had a contract to teach another year at Kingman, but I would delay signing it until I heard from him. The day came when I had to sign on for another year, or the board would assume I wasn't returning. To be safe, I signed the contract and gave it to Mr. Joy, saying, "Well, Sir, it looks like I'm here for at least another year."

I knew Carroll was disappointed that I wasn't offered a contract by Mingus Union, but she understood many teachers apply for available teaching jobs. A few days after I had returned my signed contract, Mr. Joy told me Mr. West had called him. I was to be offered a contract after all from Mingus Union.

"But, OB," I replied, "I've already signed a contract to teach here."

"Don't worry, Ernie. We'll release you if you want to go there. Mind you, I would rather you stayed here, but," he smiled, "going there will make Carroll happier."

After discussing this with her, I told OB that I'd like to go to the Verde Valley. It was a tough decision to give up a good job in Kingman to go off on a new trail to a new place. During the last few days of the school year, the faculty gave a small farewell party for the two of us who were leaving. Their good wishes made going a little tougher on me, but Carroll was extremely happy. Over the years, I learned to love the Verde Valley as much as she did.

> "What lies behind us and what lies before us are tiny matters compared to what lies within us,"
> Oliver Wendell Holmes (1841-1935).

Chapter 6

Before 1958, Mingus High School consisted only of Clarkdale and Jerome students and was located in Clarkdale. Cottonwood joined with them in 1958, and it became Mingus Union High School. The first couple of years of Mingus Union were spent in Clarkdale buildings. The move to the larger abandoned school buildings in Jerome was made because the student body became too large for Clarkdale's facility.

Before school started, Mr. Ryan, the principal, took the new members of the faculty through each of the buildings explaining where our classrooms would be. Above the "new gym" (built in 1936), was the music room. The old gym (built in 1914) located in Building A, had a balcony around it where spectators sat to watch basketball players run up and down on the small court before the new gym was built. Now that area would be used for assemblies and dramatic productions.

Building B was for Industrial Arts on the ground level, and the cafeteria was on the upper level. While we were in Jerome, a constant worry was a student would fall the three stories down to the weed-infested tennis court.

Building C was for the sciences. We were told one classroom had been a hospital operating room because it had a skylight in the ceiling.

The whole campus was located on only four acres with room for parking only for teachers and buses. Nearly 100% of the students were to be bussed up to Jerome. Many people thought it was good because there would not be students driving recklessly to school every day.

Mingus Union, located in Jerome in four buildings, was built before the First World War. It was located, however, in a beautiful location—high on Mingus Mountain overlooking most of the beautiful Verde Valley. It drew students from Jerome (not many because it was nearly a ghost town), Clarkdale, Cottonwood, Cornville, Page Springs, and the Yavapai side of Sedona. The student body numbered a few less than 400 in 1960. Walking around its halls, I looked at the graduation pictures of students who graduated from Jerome High during the last 30 or 40 years. I felt a sense of history as their eyes seemed to look down on an old but newly refurbished school. The mines in Jerome had closed down eight years before, and most of the population was relocated in other mining towns such as Bisbee, Morenci and San Manuel.

The first faculty meeting took place in the library a few days before Labor Day. The superintendent, Keith West, and the principal, Mick Ryan, made a few remarks welcoming and introducing the teachers who were new to the system.

I was assigned a big classroom near the main entrance on the second level. I taught my English students there and moved to a much smaller, darker closet-like room for Journalism. Again, we were to put out a paper with an old-fashioned mimeograph machine.

We were on a flexible schedule. Each class was an hour and a half, but we met with each only four days a week. We skipped one of our classes each day. I thought it was a great schedule, and I believe we stayed on it the entire 12 years we were in Jerome. All in all, I liked the campus, and most of my memories of school there are happy ones.

However, since the buildings had been built so long ago, many of the classrooms had no electrical outlets. To show a movie on the third floor, teachers had to have many long extension cords hooked together that would sneak through the hall and down the stairs. A lesson here is teachers must be flexible enough to "make do" under less than ideal conditions.

Carroll's parents gave us a lot to build a house in Cornville. Her dad, Curt Cornelison, was an old railroader who became a contractor and farmer. Her mother was a native Arizonan born in Oatman, another ghost town, located very near Kingman.

She became the postmaster in Cornville a couple of years after we moved into our house.

We were staying in their rental until we could build our own house. Again, we found it would be difficult to get financing, but we kept looking until we found a contractor from Sedona who was currently out of work. He agreed to build our house if I worked as part of his crew and would be responsible for painting it outside and inside. When we moved in a few days before school started, our mortgage was for 20 years, and our house payment was $73 a month. During the nearly 25 years we lived there, we added a carport, family room with a fireplace and an additional bedroom. We obtained the plans for it from a neighbor who found them in the Phoenix newspaper. We were happy there, and I don't believe we locked the front door until our daughter Janet was a freshman in high school—about 17 years from the time we first moved in.

It was about 17 miles for me to drive to Jerome and because of the "high" price of gas (around 20 cents a gallon), the teachers felt we should carpool. We did, and about five of us took turns for a week at a time. Carpooling helped to make room in the parking lot as well as helping our budgets. I was delighted I was to make about $500 more at Mingus than I was scheduled for in Kingman. I was also delighted my town newspaper duty wasn't necessary because the owner/editor, Bill Cameron, asked, "Why should we pay you to advertise for the high school? We have a reporter for that."

Little did I know at that time I would end up doing the same thing for the *Verde Independent* free that I had done for the Kingman paper for which I got 10 cents an inch. Bill Cameron was a very good man and produced a very good paper. His two wonderful daughters were a credit to Mingus and good friends with my daughter.

From the first day, I saw the teachers had a high level of *esprit de corps*. We had a large faculty room on the ground floor in Building A. It was large enough to accommodate many teachers and helped draw us together. In that room, there were chalk boards, a refrigerator and a hot plate. The morale of the staff was higher than any I ever saw or ever would see in all my years of teaching. I believe our laughing together helped draw the students in with us.

Tom Henry's classroom was located next to mine. He was a very effective math teacher with a great sense of humor. I was across the hall from the library which also served as a study hall. Jim MacLarney, my co-English teacher, was next to the library. He often said he was the "iron fist" and I was an "iron fist with a velvet glove." Everyone on the second floor, except for me, was a veteran at Mingus, and, again, I looked to them for help and advice. Mac was a New Yorker who had graduated from Providence College, a private Catholic University. He had much more of a classical education than did anyone else. He was also the drama teacher. During one of our years—I've forgotten which—Jim came to me saying he had just devoted a lot of time with his senior class to teach them how to take notes, a skill they'd need in college. Since they were all preparing for college after high school, he felt this training would be very beneficial. He asked if we could trade classes for a time, so I could lecture on English Literature much as a college professor would do. I thought this would be interesting for both of our classes to have different teachers for awhile. I was to lecture his group for three days a week while giving them reading assignments from the English literature book. Since he had more of a tendency to scare pupils, I could tell my class was relieved to have me back, if only for two days a week. I'm sure his class was relieved to have two days a week off from any school work in spite of being in Mac's classroom. When the experiment was over, both classes indicated they not only profited from it, but it was fun to have a different teacher in the room. Jim had given his students free time when they didn't have a lecture from me, so they would feel more like they were in a college class. I think both Jim and I felt that giving the pupils something a bit different for a few weeks was beneficial, and I think teachers today should consider doing something like this. It could "open" some minds of the students to examine subjects from different perspectives.

> "School buildings mirror our educational concepts. America has a predilection for straight lines, rectangles, squared-off blocks, and nowhere is this more true than in the usual school house," Lloyd Trump

Chapter 7

During my initial interview, Mr. West said, "You'll never be called on to coach an athletic team because we have plenty of coaches." However, Bill Cameron from the *Verde Independent* called me the day of the first football game and asked me to write the story *for that game only*. Each week of the season, he made this request until I began writing the stories automatically without his asking. His reporter didn't know anything about sports or really anything else. This unpaid job was an avenue for me to get to know Hank Barbarick and Bob Richmond, the football coaches better. They became very good friends of mine as a result. During the spring of my first year at Mingus, I was called into Mr. West's office. Hank was with him, and before many words were spoken, I thought, *Oh, oh. I hope they don't want me to coach anything*.

Mr. West began the conference by saying, "Hank thinks there will be enough boys out for football next fall to justify a JV team. Will you consider being its coach for <u>only</u> one year? We can get you $200 more on your next contract if you will." Since that money would amount to about a dollar a day, it wasn't the money that motivated me to say I would. To this day, I don't know why I agreed, but I did. However, the year turned into about ten. I confess now that I had a good time as JV coach even though I gave up many Saturdays to do it. My son, Mike, learned to love football and sports as he practically became a member of the teams while he was growing up.

My sole aim while coaching was to make the game fun for the players. All the squad played in most of the games, and they learned a bit about the game such as learning how to put on hip pads to knowing what a multiple offense was. I was never pressured to win as perhaps, the varsity coach was.

I firmly believe that when kids go out for sports or engage in other high school activities, they are more apt to study harder in the academic classroom. Many of my "Gabe's babes" have come back over the years saying playing football for Mingus was very important in their lives. Over time the JV games began to draw so many fans that we started to charge admission.

Take my word for it; a teacher has to have good memories about his job to take with him into retirement. The years I spent coaching provide many of those memories.

There were many boys and games I remember better than others. One Saturday afternoon we played Prescott High. During the whole of the afternoon, we virtually camped on their goal line, but didn't score. The Badgers beat us 6-0. The rest of the weekend, I spent trying to figure a way to convince the young Marauders that scoring was important. On the way to practice the next Monday afternoon, I stopped at the only Clarkdale bar and borrowed their silver container that was used to chill champagne. I also purchased several big bottles of 7-Up, some paper cups and a sack of ice. I got these things into the locker room without being seen with them. After we left the locker building to go onto the practice field, Gary Peterson, our manager, was to take these things out to the sideline and put them on a table after we started scrimmaging. Finally our offense scored a touchdown. Both coaches jumped up and down with joy, and yelled at them "Isn't crossing the goal line wonderful? Come over and let's celebrate by having a drink of champagne."

I don't know if that unorthodox lesson made a difference or not, but we always scored after that. I do know, however, many boys came to me over the years saying they had fun in football, and the best part was that little party after we got shut out by Prescott. I'm not sure if Mr. Harkey, the head coach of the varsity, totally approved of this approach when he came down to our end of the field to ask, "What's going on down here?" But he smiled when I told him it was a celebration for having scored. I think the little party helped bond our players to our school. I also think it pays the teacher to "think outside the box" on occasion. There are sometimes more important lessons than those prescribed by the curriculum.

Many kids began playing sports at Mingus by being on the JV football team, and I remember them all. I especially remember our manager—Gary Peterson. He loved his job and wished he could play. However, he couldn't play because of asthma. Everyone on the team—no, everyone in school loved him because he loved life so much. He died before he graduated, and his folks left some money to be used for a scholarship for someone who showed exceptional courage. Those who won this scholarship were prouder of it than any other award they received.

A very nice boy named Serafin Razo remains in my memory because he loved the game so much he often made mistakes in his enthusiasm. He was a very speedy halfback, but too often went to the wrong side of the line where he didn't receive proper blocking. He just couldn't run to the right hole. All the coaches worked with him, but he continually ran to the left side when the play called was to the right.

One day he came to practice with a band-aid on his right hand near his thumb. As the team broke the huddle, the quarterback whispered, "Serafin, run to the band-aid side." Sometimes he was told to run to the side without the band-aid. That worked, and from then on, we saw to it Serafin always wore a band-aid on one hand.

When I watch college or pro ball on TV, I imagine the players are 12 and 13 running up and down our football field. Imagining that is a lot more fun than just watching the real players. Great memories often come from extracurricular activities. Again, teachers must build memories while they teach.

> "We are what we repeatedly do. Excellence, therefore, is not an act but a habit," Aristotle

Chapter 8

S ome exciting things happened to me and to Mingus during the first years of the 1960s. At a faculty meeting one day, Mr. West informed us we were going to be evaluated by the North Central Accrediting Committee. Being evaluated by people from all over the state was scary as well as causing a lot of extra work. We all had many forms to fill out for the various committees who would carefully read our statements of what we were doing and then judge us on how well we were doing it. The faculty had many meetings after school to make sure we included everything in the forms. This was the first time Mingus was evaluated by outsiders to give us accreditation. If we passed, our students would be deemed more worthy of scholarships to colleges. Our faculty room would be closed to us for the three days of the committee's visit because it would be the committee's workroom. The big day finally arrived. About 25 serious looking strangers came—the

North Central committee would determine if our school was doing the job or not. We noticed there were both men and women in the group, and all of them were dressed in their Sunday best. The faculty also dressed formally—attempting to meet the challenge and impress the visitors.

Dr. Dan Bright, a member of the school board, gave Georgia Franklin, the school secretary, a bottle of nerve-calming pills, so teachers could use them if they wanted or needed them. When the 8 o'clock bell rang on the first day, I was sweating and trembling a bit as I took roll. Just as I finished, there was a knock on the door, and a man came in with a clipboard. He asked, "Are you Mr. Ernest Gabrielson, and do you mind if I come and see your class in action?"

I shook hands for the first time with Dr. Louie MacDonald. His big smile put me at ease as he looked all around the classroom. Then he spoke to the students. He told them he had been a student in this very room while attending Jerome High School. He then continued telling them he had begun his teaching career in this same room. He joked about some of the things that happened to him as a student and teacher. He decided after a few years of teaching here, he would become a principal and later superintendent of Jerome High. He made my students laugh a lot as his stories were both funny and interesting. Then the class-change bell rang and Louie turned to me and said, "Well, Mr. Gabrielson, you must be a very good teacher because the period seemed very short." He and his clipboard walked out of my class that day, but Louie never walked out of my life. He was a very-respected instructor at NAU, and after that visit, he came to Mingus often. Years later when I took a class from him, I discovered he often used Mingus Union as an example of a well-run school.

The whole faculty found every member of the committee striving to make their visit as pleasant as possible. For me, Dr. MacDonald's visit set the tone, and I was at ease when other evaluators came into my classroom or quizzed us about the English Department.

It was a wonderful day when we found we had not only passed but passed with flying colors. While North Central was visiting us, the students were magnificent. Many of them were interviewed about their feelings and thoughts on their school; and they, too, indicated their pride.

One recommendation of the committee was soon we would need a new facility with more space.

Shortly after all the visitors left, some less exciting but important things came to our school. Everyone's favorite mythical student enrolled the day we gave standardized tests. These are the ones test takers mark with a pencil on answer sheets. Then the answer sheets are sent away to be electronically scored. Those tests were given to find out how our students fared against national averages.

On test day during the noon hour, our faculty room was crowded. Fred Peck, a biology teacher with a sense of humor, found a blank answer sheet and asked, "I wonder what would happen if I just marked this randomly. Maybe it would have a higher score than some of our students."

When Fred finished marking the paper and was about to throw it away, I said, "Fred, you need to put a name on the paper." Then I added, "Let's use Norman Farquhar." It was the name of a character on the then popular *Bull Winkle* TV show. We all laughed as Fred put the name on the answer sheet. I then said, "I'm going to mark him absent fifth period." Tom Henry smiled and added he would mark him absent sixth period. Norman would then be absent all afternoon.

About half way through the fifth period, the attendance officer came to my room. Mrs. Tittle said, "Ernie, you marked a Norman Farquhar absent. There is no one by that name registered here."

With as serious a face as I could muster, "Mrs. Tittle, he sits right over there." I pointed to an empty desk and asked the whole class, "Does anyone know why Norman Farquhar is absent this afternoon?" To their credit, most of the class shook their heads without laughing. A boy said "I think his mother came and picked him up." Mrs. Tittle left after giving me a funny look while scratching her head as she turned away. I would give a lot to know what she was thinking then. After she left, the class broke out into laughter.

During the few minutes between fifth and sixth periods, I walked by the office, and Mrs. Franklin called me in. She had opened all the drawers of her files to show me there was no Norman Farquhar registered. I couldn't hide my smile as I told her Tittle was looking all over for him, and he'd also be absent from Mr. Henry's sixth-period class.

She laughed and said, "You guys are going to drive Tittle mad. You need to tell her you made Norman up."

That was how Norman came to Mingus. Whenever a picture was taken of members of teams or activities, we named the students, but always inserted, "Not pictured, Norman Farquhar." But he really became an icon with the student body by his appearance on the field before a football game against Marana.

My fifth period Honors English class finished their work and we started plotting. Someone suggested it would be a good idea for Norman to be at the game that night. Margaret Broughton volunteered to wrap herself up in bandages and get a crutch to run across the field before the game acting the part of an injured player. It was my job to fix it with Chuck Mabery, the PA announcer, to announce, "We are sorry to inform you Norman Farquhar, a star Marauder player, was slightly injured in an auto accident this afternoon, but he is here to cheer his Marauders on to victory tonight." Then Margaret ran across the field. The cheering and laughter of our student body was as loud then as it ever got. Before Chuck could announce it was a joke, Margaret threw away her crutch and ran toward the Mingus pregame huddle. Someone mentioned he saw the whole Marana team take off their helmets and hold them over their hearts because they, too, thought it was serious.

Norman showed up many times as part of our student body. He even went down the hill from Jerome to Cottonwood when the new school opened. Sadly, he was lost as Mingus High School grew more sophisticated with a student body which had grown to over a thousand. I hope Norman enjoyed being part of our school as much as the students enjoyed him. He did a lot to bond our students and faculty.

> "A sense of humor . . . is needed armor. Joy in one's heart and some laughter on one's lips is a sign that the person down deep has a pretty good grasp of life," Hugh Sidey

Chapter 9

As I write this, I wish I could return to Cottonwood to drink coffee with my fellow teachers who taught in Jerome. I need a spur to my memory as I try to recall the teachers and students who made Mingus High a great place to be. Even "snow days" were fun when the buses and cars couldn't make it up the hill to Jerome, and we all had a free day—after some of the students pelted our stalled cars with snow balls.

But I do remember some of the things we did making going to work fun. I remember well the day when a class came in after having biology with Mr. Peck. They were delighted to tell me about Mr. Peck walking around the room lecturing when an announcement came over the loud speaker which was above the chalk board. "Without pausing in his speech, Mr. Peck picked up the long window pole and knocked the speaker right off the wall." It was also reported he didn't pause a moment but just went on talking.

One Friday afternoon we had finished the lesson and were sitting around concocting a joke we could play on Mr. MacLarney. When a student asked if she could go to the office to sharpen her pencil, someone had an idea. "Since we don't have a sharpener in this room, she should go down the hall to ask Mr. MacLarney if she could use his." I sent her down to his room, and after she left, I asked about five others to quietly walk down the hall and, one at a time, go in and ask him *politely* if it was all right to use his sharpener. Eventually, my whole class was lined up in the hall giggling and waiting to sharpen their pencils in Mac's room. I was standing outside my classroom laughing when Tom Henry came out and signaled me to turn around. When I did, Superintendent West was standing there watching our antics. "What's going on, Mr. Gabrielson?"

"I'll explain later, Mr. West." With a red face, I signaled, "Come on back!" My class came back all anxious to tell about Mac's reaction when they entered his room. One said, "At first he was angry, but then he saw we were joking."

Of course, the joking went both ways. I was late returning to my class one day; and when I walked in, there was no one there. I went next door to ask Tom Henry if he'd seen my class. He said, "No," but I looked carefully around just in case they were hiding on the floor. Right in front of all his students he remarked, "You've got no class, Mr. Gabrielson?" I went back to my room and sat at my desk confident I was the butt of a joking teacher—but which one? One of my students who was also late came in and asked, "Where's the class, Mr. Gabrielson?"

I replied, "I don't really know."

The student—I forget who—went to his desk and started to cry. I was beginning to grow concerned as well when Mac came in and asked, "Did you lose something, Ernie?" He was sporting a big grin.

Then my class came straggling in laughing. They had been hiding in Mac's room. Since Mac knew I'd be a little late getting to class, he came up and requested my students to come to his room.

On April Fool's Day, we wanted a plot which would involve the whole school. I suggested after the students were all seated in their next period, an announcement would be made saying, "Today is the anniversary of the date the U.S Congress made Arizona a territory, and everyone should stand, face Washington, and observe a moment of silence." I went downstairs to ask if it would be all right to make the announcement because it was the day of jokes. The message was to be sent at exactly 2:00 p.m., a few minutes after the start of the next period.

Right on time, the announcement was made exactly as written. My students, who weren't in on the joke, rose up and were clearly confused as to which way to face. After a minute or so, the office announced, "APRIL FOOL!"

The next day the class which dreamed up the joke, delightedly talked about what had happened in their various classes when the announcement came. One student was sent by Miss Evans to the office for being "disrespectful" because he had laughed. She called him back after realizing it was a joke.

Jim MacLarney, having studied classics as well as drama in college was putting on the famous Greek tragedy *Antigone*. He was very serious about this since he often said he wanted to bring classics to the Verde Valley. He maintained our "cowboy" culture didn't know about the great classics of ancient Greece. Of course, he being an eastern boy from an extremely prestigious private college had studied classical literature more intensely than most of us. One day in the faculty room, Fred Peck asked, "Jim, when is Aunty Gone going to be on? Is it some play about distant relatives?"

Jim retorted angrily, "It's an-**tig**-*uh*-nee, a Greek tragedy!" He pronounced every syllable slowly.

From then on, every teacher including Merle Crawford and Mory Clark, our two oldest teachers who really didn't play many jokes, called, it "Aunty Gone." Fred, a wonderful artist, drew a picture of "Auntie" walking away from a house waving goodbye while someone in the house asked, "Is Auntie gone?" The faculty room, being an old classroom, had chalk boards always sporting a Fred Peck original drawing to amuse the teachers.

John O'Donnell came into the room for lunch one day and reached into the refrigerator for his sack lunch. He bit into a sandwich and discovered it tasted very bad. He looked under the bread and saw two pieces of paper—one labeled ham and the other labeled cheese. Mr. Henry asked quickly, "Is something the matter, John?"

The cheerleader sponsor came in one morning dragging a very long piece of butcher paper which she hung above the chalk board. On it was very artistically painted letters spelling MARAUDERS. She asked, "How do you like this? We're taking it to the game tonight, and the players coming onto the field will run through it as the band plays the fight song."

I couldn't resist and replied, "It would be fine if MARAUDER was spelled right." I kept a straight face, but it was hard to do.

About to faint, as Garee Wombacher looked at it, she asked, "It's spelled right, isn't it, Jim?" She trusted Mac's knowledge of spelling a little more than she did mine apparently.

"It's okay, Garee. You only left out one letter, but maybe no one will notice." She was starting to cry when Mory Clark told her the spelling was right. "They were just pulling your leg."

We carpooled to school, and one of the pool members was Bill Hall, an Industrial Arts teacher. One day he had to umpire a softball game and left school early to go down to a Cottonwood baseball diamond. He was very proud of his car. In fact, he christened it "Pink Lady" and always spoke of his car as if it were a beautiful, live woman. He gave the keys to Tom Henry to drive us home after school—a big mistake. As we left the parking lot, we carried with us a bunch of scrap metal and discarded auto parts. When we hit the road next to the park, we all threw the metal out of the car from the side Bill couldn't see from the field. We wanted it to appear to him as if his wonderful lady was falling apart. We pulled over and raced back to pick up the fallen parts of beautiful "Pink Lady." While Bill watched us in horror, the expression on his face brought on lots of laughter. We all hoped that incident wasn't the biggest reason causing him to seek employment in Tucson. He often said he and his wife wanted to go to a place with a miniature golf course.

Bill was also a bit of a jokester. One day a lens fell out of his glasses. During class, with the lens in his pocket, he pulled out his handkerchief while talking and ran it through the empty space as if polishing it. He said the kids reacted as if he were crazy.

Probably Tom Henry initiated more tricks to tickle our funny bones than anyone else. However, most of the faculty did some funny things from time to time.

Since Mac was very Irish, Tom gave us all a bit of orange to irritate him since he wore a lot of green on St. Patrick's Day. Even many of the students got something orange to wear after they saw us wearing it.

One of our counselors, Elizabeth Fitzgerald, had a sore on her nose once and put a band-aid over it. Tom issued all of us band-aids to wear. Many students went to the school nurse and wore them just like the teachers. I never knew about Fitzgerald's sense of humor, but she never again wore anything on her nose.

On a more serious note, laughter works well to lessen anxiety. Nearly everyone alive at the time remembers the day President Kennedy was shot in 1963. During the period before lunch, I sent a boy down to the office for something, and when he came back, his face was ashen. He said, "Someone shot the President! It was on the radio in the office!" I asked for details, but he had nothing to add, except the President had been taken to Parkman Hospital in Dallas. When the bell rang for the lunch hour, there was little talk as everyone waited for news. Then it was announced the President had died. In addition, Mr. West announced after our fifth-hour class, the buses would take everyone home. School was to be suspended for the next several days—at least until after the funeral.

As my students were filing quietly into my fifth period classroom, I noticed every girl was sobbing tearfully, and the boys were all extremely somber. I have no idea now what my lesson plan was, but I knew I had to change it. No regular lesson would be effective, so I decided to read Mark Twain's *The Celebrated Jumping Frog of Calaveras County* to them. I started to read amid the sounds of crying, but as the story progressed, I began to hear some tentative giggling. Later in the story, the giggling turned to laughter. By the end of the story, and blessedly, at the end of the period, the somber mood was at least temporarily gone. There were times in the story I had to stop reading because I was laughing too. Out in the hall, Tom Henry asked what I had done in my class to cause laughter. I explained about reading Twain's story. I think, perhaps, my reading it aloud was one of my best lessons.

During the next few days, the whole world was saddened as TV showed the funeral. It was a heart-breaking period in our lives. Many athletic contests were postponed or cancelled throughout the nation.

"A good laugh overcomes more difficulties and dissipates more dark clouds than any other one thing," Laura Ingalls Wilder

Chapter 10

When I think back to those Jerome days, I am reminded of how journalism at Mingus changed. During the summer after our first year in Jerome, several of our teaching staff car-pooled to NAU for summer classes. MacLarney and I took a class in Journalism. I met several journalism teachers there from around the state, and we compared notes.

When fall came, I was asked to supervise the production of our yearbook as well as producing the school newspaper. I had recruited some students who were interested in journalism, so the class was more interesting and we produced better papers than the first year.

Because of the class's double-duty, we were allowed to use a large room on the third floor. However, we still used the mimeograph machine and had to carry stencils down to it. We were also producing football programs which we all maintained should bring us at least a dime each, but we gave them away. My students worked hard to meet deadlines for the yearbook and to produce a worthy newspaper even though it was mimeographed.

Then something bad happened which turned our class completely around. On his way down to the mimeograph machine, a student scratched a filthy word on one of the stencils. It was so small it was overlooked. A few minutes after we passed the newspaper out, Jim MacLarney came into my class and whispered, "Ernie, we have to go around and collect the papers." He showed me the words the student had scratched on it. We both ran around collecting as many of the papers as we could. At least if parents became angry, we could report we tried to get them all.

The next day, as I started into the journalism class, a boy met me at the door and confessed he had done the scratching. He was extremely sorry and offered to drop the class, but after we talked for awhile, I told him to take his seat. I opened the class by announcing we had produced our last mimeographed newspaper, and from now on, it would be printed.

"But that's expensive," came a voice from the front row, "how do we pay for it?"

I replied, "We'll sell advertising and hope the *Verde Independent* will help us by doing it within our budget.

If truth be told, it wasn't the first time I had thought we deserved a printed paper. I discussed this with many teachers during the summer at NAU. I particularly remember talking to Bert Bostrom and Bob Cox from the state Inter-Scholastic Press Association. I also drank coffee with a wonderful lady from Bisbee, whose paper almost always was judged the best in Arizona. Her name was Rachael Riggens. I took a semester of Journalism from her while I was in high school. She had recruited me to report on sports since her class consisted entirely of girls. (Talk about dying and going to heaven.)

I also talked to a bakery in Sedona. The owner agreed to deliver fresh doughnuts to us every day to sell. At first, I didn't realize what a gold mine I had with the doughnuts until the money started rolling in. In class, we were set to produce Mingus Union's first printed *Mingus Spirit*. The kids sold a lot of advertising as well as doughnuts. John Bell from the *Verde Independent* agreed to help us make it work. We spent a lot of time creating a masthead for the paper which would set ours apart. Jokingly, I suggested we use a drawing of our wonderful view of the valley and have a slogan saying, "We look down on everyone." Then I had to spend a lot of time talking my class out of it.

As we were writing stories, I soon discovered the class, consisting mostly of girls, was weak when it came to sports. We got through the year fine, but I knew I had to do something to interest some of our best student athletes to take journalism. There was a very pretty cheerleader in one of my English classes. On the day when the kids pre-registered for the next year, I stopped her at the door and asked, "Cindy, would you please take journalism next year?"

She laughed and said, "Mr. Gabrielson, you know I can't write good enough for the paper."

"Cindy, there are a number of jobs you can do for us. We need good people to sell advertising and do some other things."

"Okay, Mr. Gabrielson, but don't expect me to do much writing."

Then I went to a few boys and subtly mentioned Cindy was going to take Journalism. We enrolled a few boys to write sport stories.

I've always felt a twinge of guilt using Cindy to help recruit, but she proved to be an excellent seller of advertising and was an asset in other ways.

Norman Farquhar graced the pages a good bit but was never pictured. Bob Richmond's basketball team gave us our best banner headline. We won the state championship and our headline was simply:

We're the Champs!

"The whole art of teaching is only the art of awakening the natural curiosity of the mind for the purpose of satisfying it afterwards,"
Anatole France

Chapter 11

After we attended the NAU journalism course and began to print the paper, journalism became much better. We no longer had to recruit good students because they began to sign up without any urging from me. Some even signed up for a second year as an elective. The second-year students said they were going to major in journalism at college, and they became mentors for those new to my journalism class. For the first time, we spent a bit of class time studying the history, ethics, and power of the press. In order to measure ourselves against papers from other schools in Arizona, we exchanged papers with them. Our editors scanned these papers searching out new ideas for editorials, feature stories, and photography. The students wanted to join *Quill and Scroll,* an honor society for high school journalists. Because of this, I called Bert Bostrom, the president of the Arizona branch, and asked him for help. He said he would initiate my students into the society, and he would arrange the whole thing. When he and a few other journalism teachers arrived from Phoenix, he asked us to have a brief all-school assembly to watch the ceremony. They did a great job of taking our students into the society by giving them pins as well as having them take an oath to practice journalism responsibly. The ceremony was fabulous since they even had part of it lit up by candlelight. Many non-journalism students became very proud of our school and our paper.

We began to have fun sending our paper to the national and state organizations which judged quality. The paper I wanted my students to beat was the one from Bisbee because it was the state champion, and its wonderful guiding light was my high school teacher.

One day at noon, some of the ceiling plaster in the bookstore fell down on some students' heads. No one was hurt, but I thought it might be a small feature story. I asked a girl to go to the bookstore and write a story about it. Her reply was, "Mr. Gabrielson, everyone already knows about it. No one needs to write a story about it."

I snapped back a little sharply, "No one knows a damn thing until they read it in our paper. Go get the story!" It was then I learned the true meaning of the word, *flounce*. The girl *flounced* out of the room armed with a pencil and a note pad. A few minutes later, she *flounced* back in and began writing. When the bell rang, she again *flounced* up to my desk and put her story there as she left. Sadly, I can't remember her name. During the class change, I picked it up and read it. The story began, "Chicken Little was right. The sky is falling." The story went on to its finish, and I marked it for typing it for use in the next issue. The next day the girl had forgotten her anger and was eager for a new assignment. That story, by the way, was judged the best feature story in Arizona journalism that year. The writer became a waitress at a restaurant we often visited, and I never failed to tell her how she had taught me the true meaning of *flounce*. She always laughed and said, "Well, Chicken Little was right, wasn't she?"

Another lesson I remember well was one no teacher today could do because he might get fired or even arrested. But this happened before many of our modern-day fears.

I was teaching the importance of the lead paragraph in a news story. I emphasized one must be very careful with it, being sure the *who, what, where, when* and *why* were not based on assumption, because the lead had to be accurate. I wanted something to really bring the lesson home to my 20 young journalists.

After securing the superintendent's permission, I got the blank cartridge pistol which was used on the football field to signal the end of quarters. I asked for help from Jim MacLarney and Fred Peck. They both had a free period the hour journalism met. My room had an old-fashioned cloak room to one side and a door leading into it from the hall. It was mainly used to store janitorial supplies. I told my "actors" I wanted Fred to run into my room exactly 20 minutes after the period began and do some shouting about being chased by Mr. MacLarney who had the gun. We spent 19 minutes going over the lesson on being totally accurate with the lead story and never basing the lead on assumptions.

Then Fred burst into the room, shouting, "Ernie, help me! Jim's after me with a gun!" Then he ran into the cloakroom. Seconds later Jim came in waving the pistol and shouting, "I saw him come in here! Where is he?"

They both ran out into the hall through the cloak room where Jim gave Fred the gun which he fired. I could see my journalists were stunned by the show, but my smile showed them it was all an act. To this day, I thank my lucky stars none of them fainted. I asked them to write the lead for a news story including most of the "Ws."

When they turned them in and I read them, I said, "You all flunked. Mr. Peck was the one who fired the shot, not Mr. MacLarney." They all looked properly chagrined, but they all indicated for years the lesson was a great one. I wish I had given my "actors" an academy award. They were good.

During the 100-year storm of 1967, we had finished getting the Christmas issue ready at the newspaper office downtown. We were going to pass it out the last day before Christmas vacation, but the storm cancelled the school two days before. Those who remember the storm will recall no traffic could move for several days around the Verde Valley. I was proud of two of my students who collected the paper and delivered it on "horseback." The radio station announced students could pick up the Christmas edition of the *Mingus Spirit* at several locations in Cottonwood and Clarkdale. That was dedication, and I remember it lovingly.

During the storm, it snowed so much the roofs of the businesses downtown were in danger of caving in. This was also true of many of the older houses. The radio announced many boys from the high school would come to the places in danger and shovel the snow off the roofs. They worked at this for several days helping people who needed help. I was very proud of them and I think of those boys when people criticize the youth of today.

One last thing: At the end of the year, several of my students and I attended the award ceremony in Tempe of the Arizona Inter-scholastic Press Association. We had an opportunity to meet staffs from all over Arizona and enjoyed looking at many of the displays during the morning and early afternoon. This, by the way, was when we learned our Chicken Little story was judged the best feature story in the state. The last item on the agenda was to name and award the top three papers in Arizona. "Third place," announced the President of the association "goes to . . ." He named some school in Phoenix. "Second place goes to the *Copper Chronicle* from Bisbee High."

I whispered to my students, "Let's go now and beat the crowd."

Then the announcement came, "And the paper we judged best in the state is the *Mingus Spirit* from Mingus Union High School." We were all so stunned and flabbergasted no one rose to go up to receive the award. Finally two of our girls went up there, crying with happiness and accepted the award.

We were very happy returning to Cottonwood. Our first stop was at Superintendent West's house where we all stood on his front porch and told him we were judged the best newspaper in Arizona.

He congratulated us all showing he was very proud of us. When the students went back to the car, I said, "Mr. West, I've taught journalism for seven years here. I think we need to relieve me and get someone else. Please consider this."

The next year, we had a new journalism instructor, and I went back to my first loves—teaching English and Reading with a bit of history thrown in.

> "All genuine learning is active, not passive. It involves the use of the mind, not just the memory. It is a process of discovery, in which the student is the main agent, not the teacher," Mortimer J. Adler.

Chapter 12

Keith West was an excellent administer. He was thoughtful, dedicated to the best education possible, and supported his teachers. If he had one failing, and I'm not sure it's a failing, he was slow in making up his mind. One seldom got either a definitive *yes* or *no* from him. It was always something like, "I'll think about it."

One time, Jim MacLarney and I went to his office asking for something. We went in together thinking the force of numbers would be in our favor. We presented our case and listened to Keith for a few minutes in reply. As we left the office, Jim asked, "Ernie, was it a *yes* or a *no?*" I didn't know either.

Our football field in Clarkdale left something to be desired in those days. The lights were dim, and we didn't have a time clock so fans could watch and keep track of the score. The time was kept by an official on the field, and there had to be communication between the PA announcer and the official.

I was strongly in favor of obtaining an electronic scoreboard and clock for the fans' benefit. I was tired of being embarrassed by coaches and players of visiting teams who made fun of our facilities. One coach even remarked, "We should have brought our seeing-eye dogs here." Coach Harkey was pushing for a good time clock also. Keith argued since the field was in Clarkdale and not on our campus, with no real fence around it, an electronic scoreboard would be vandalized. "They are too expensive, and we won't have one until we can make it secure from vandals. Besides those things cost more than we can afford."

I won the argument—no, not me really. It was a few kids. One day before practice some raggedy kids came up to me and handed me a brand new football. "Coach, you left this on the field last night." Whether it was right or not, I gave them an older football and complimented them for their honesty. The next morning, I went into Keith's office and told him the story. He agreed we would have a new scoreboard next year.

The teachers bugged him and the principal, Hank Barbarick, to ask the board to float a bond election to build a new school in Cottonwood, but Keith moved slowly there as well. I think he was gaining ground with the board, but he warned us about moving too fast. We all knew he was working for it, but little or no progress was apparent to us.

Then we suffered a big loss. Keith accepted the superintendent's job in Kingman. When I heard this, I rushed into Hank Barbarick's office fuming and cussing. "Damn it all, Hank. He was becoming more and more convinced about floating a bond issue, and now we'll have to work on a new guy. It's like starting over."

Hank's reply was surprising. "If the teachers will back me to get the job, I'll also push for an election." Word spread quickly through the staff, and we did, indeed, support Hank. While Keith finished the year, we looked forward to Hank becoming boss. At a board meeting at the end of the year, Hank accepted the job as superintendent, and a new principal was hired. Jess Udall was very competent and effective.

On the first day of faculty meetings the next fall, several of us were driving to school in the car pool. I asked Tom Henry to nominate me for president of the local branch of the teacher's association.

"What?" Tom asked incredulously. "Do you really want that, Ernie?"

Everyone in the car was surprised because wanting to be president of MUEA was like saying, "I want to catch the measles."

I said I wanted it so I could attend <u>all</u> the board meetings and speak about building a new school. Needless to say, at our first meeting, I was elected president unanimously. My winning the election was probably because I was the only candidate.

Forgive me for interrupting the narrative with a bit of philosophy. I supported the local association including the

Arizona Education Association and the National Education Association throughout my whole teaching career. If the teachers made any progress for higher wages, the National and State Associations helped. Many people speak against teachers having the protection of tenure brought about by these groups, but I think it's good. During the depression, jobs were so scarce administrators occasionally took advantage of women teachers by threatening to fire them if they wouldn't do what the administrator wanted. Tenure simply means a teacher, after three years, has the option of a board hearing if his/her job is threatened by unfair administrators.

I have little patience with teachers who won't support the local association but take all the benefits the Association wins for them. Veteran teachers usually ask all incoming teachers to consider membership. I did not agree with everything the state or national associations supported, but membership gave me a voice to speak on the issues affecting us.

After I was elected local president, I attended every board meeting. At the time the board consisted of Mr. Pat Patterson, owner of the local feed store, Dr. Daniel Bright, Dr. Ray Pecharich, John Tavasci and Ed Moritz from Sedona. At every meeting they would ask, "Do the teachers have anything to say?" They knew they didn't really need to ask. They just looked at me getting up.

I, along with others, stood up asking the board to consider floating a bond election to build a new school. I would repeat the same arguments at each meeting. At first my suggestion was met with a smile and a comment, "It would certainly be defeated." Hank, too, usually spoke up outlining some of the problems with our old Jerome buildings. The problems, of course, were many and well—known to the board.

In spite of my happiness teaching there, those problems did hamper our efforts. Most of the students had to be transported by buses and some of our stairways were dangerous. The lighting and wiring were extremely inadequate. The school was built in 1914, a time when electrical outlets were unimportant. We always worried about the staircase leading to the cafeteria. If a student fell from there, it was a couple of hundred feet to the ground. A teacher had to be on duty to allow only a certain number of students on those stairs at a time. The teacher also monitored the line. Once when Tom Henry was on duty, a student named Sparky cut the line so he could be next. Tom caught him and sent him clear back to the end of the line. The student glared at Tom and said, "All right, Mr. Henry. I just won't eat lunch." This was spoken with just a bit of anger.

As he was stomping off, Tom said, "Sparky, you really did fix my wagon." Later, Tom came into the faculty room laughing as he told us about Sparky punishing him by not eating lunch. All of us who knew Sparky joined Tom in laughter.

One night, however, happy news came from the board meeting. They did, at last, give their approval to have the much-wanted election. They made the motion with only one dissenting vote—the member from Sedona. Dr. Bright said, "I hope this gets you off our backs, Ernie."

The next day Hank cornered me. He said, "Ernie, we've all got to work very hard to make sure the election passes. Will you go with me to every group in the Verde Valley as we push for victory? I don't think it'll pass, but who knows? We need to try."

I replied, "I would like to go with you and talk to the voters." Going in, we knew we would face an uphill battle in Jerome, Clarkdale, and Sedona. We needed lots of votes in Cottonwood, Page Springs and Cornville to pass it. When Hank and I Left school to campaign, one teacher said, "There they go—the Hank and Ernie Show."

During the campaign, I felt discouraged at times and even went to Bisbee to talk to my old Kingman Superintendent, O.B. Joy, asking, "If our bond issue election fails, can I have a job in Bisbee? I'd love to teach for you again, and I love your new high school."

He assured me I could. Jack Miller, my old history teacher was principal then, and he took me on a tour of Bisbee's new high school in Warren, the place where I grew up. My wife didn't smile much about the prospect because she didn't want to leave the Verde Valley. I think she worked harder for the bond issue than most of us in fear of having to move.

Hank would schedule teachers to cover my classes if we arranged for a few voters to meet and listen to our pitch. We talked about a "community school" which would be open to all citizens. I know the entire faculty worked diligently for its passage, but we were not optimistic about our chances.

Besides our worry about the bond issue, we lost Elmer Garcia and Fred Peck. They both took jobs at Eastern Colorado College at Gunnison, Colorado. Both of these teachers had been part of our wonderful faculty at Jerome and we felt a great loss. We all remembered Elmer's story about his first meeting with his baseball squad. He said he worked very hard to introduce himself with perfect English, but he closed his first meeting by saying, "Everybody, get on your feets."

> "I never allow myself to become discouraged under any circumstances . . . The three great essentials to achieve anything worthwhile are, first, hard work; second, stick-to-itiveness; third, common sense," Thomas A. Edison

Chapter 13

Looking back, we knew the various communities in the Valley were sorely divided on the bond issue. However, our staff came together as never before. We all pasted "VOTE YES," on our cars. I smile as I remember one day when I went to Clarkdale and stopped at the Clarkdale News Stand. I parked on Main Street right in front with my car covered with signs saying, "VOTE YES" on every window. There was a bar in the front with a pool table and some chairs and tables in back. As I walked in, I felt a little like some bad guy in western movies. The conversations had been loud and jovial before I entered, but all that stopped when they saw me. I remember enjoying those few minutes as I ordered a beer and drank it slowly while sitting at the bar. "How's it going, Ed?" I asked Ed Starkey on the other side of the bar. I knew Ed couldn't take a position since his customers represented both sides.

"Okay, Ernie. I hope everything is going good with you."

I don't honestly think there was another word spoken while I was there. When I left, I could hear the din of conversations renewed.

After the polls closed on Election Day, we all waited anxiously for the result. Hank, some of the board, and many teachers stayed in the Cottonwood city building. I don't think there was much conversation among us while we listened to the local radio station for news. The first results came from Jerome since there were so few voters who lived there. The issue was voted down by a huge majority. This is understandable since if the vote passed for the bonds, Jerome would lose the school. Many of its businesses would also be hurt if the school moved down to Cottonwood.

Then the results came from Clarkdale. It was the same story. We lost by many votes. Again, if it passed, the school district there would lose the high school. There were few smiles as we waited for the results to come in from the other three areas. We all became a little happier when the radio indicated Cornville and Page Springs had voted for the bond big time.

We knew we'd lose in Sedona but wondered by how much. Then the results came from there. We lost, but not by as much as we thought we would. We had many students from West Sedona, and I believe they campaigned hard for the bond passage. Then the vote came in from Cottonwood. We received so many votes from there the bond issue was a success!

I can't recall what was done after we had the news, but I know I hugged Hank and many of the teachers. I'm not sure if my feet touched the ground for several hours as we celebrated. There was no one happier than Carroll, who now didn't face the prospect of moving down to Bisbee.

"I guess you won't be going to Bisbee," one of the teachers said as we shook hands and grinned at each other.

"I guess not," I answered as I hugged my smiling wife.

Not long after the election, the board met with several architects who had beautiful pictures of schools which they had designed and some sketches of their ideas for the new high school. I have forgotten their names, but three or four land developers came together and gave the district over 60 acres in the Southeast corner of Cottonwood. That was a most splendid gift! To this day that gift reminds me about many wonderful people who put schools ahead of personal riches.

At that time, we could only spend money our assessed valuation permitted—we only had $1.4 million to work with. That sounds like very little today, but we had to make it work. The gift of the land made it possible to build our new Mingus Union but without many frills. We all had a good time looking over the drawings and visualizing our new school.

Bob Starkovich, an old Jerome boy, who became an architect, showed us a design we could both afford and love. He was awarded the contract to draw plans for the school. When I was allowed to speak at these sessions, I told everyone

I wanted the library to be located in the exact center of the plant, and more importantly, I wanted an open auditorium. Most auditoriums then were huge spaces which were locked up when not in use. I visualized a space with theater seats so students could use it all day, and if it were necessary, some areas could be used as classrooms. (We did use sections of the auditorium at times as classrooms.)

One day, I was walking down the hall when the principal, Jess Udall, stopped me. He told me he had resigned as principal to take a job with the state department in Phoenix. Jess was an extremely nice guy and a good principal.

I wondered who would replace him but was not worrying about it too much. Then Hank called me into his office and said he wanted me to be principal.

"When Hell freezes over, Hank," I said. "Not me! I'm an English teacher."

"Ernie, if you want some say in what the new school is going to look like, you need to be part of the administration."

"That's blackmail, Hank."

"I guess it is. Talk it over with Carroll and give me an answer soon."

I didn't want to leave the classroom to be principal. I loved teaching too much, but I wanted our new school to have some of the things I had seen in various new school buildings around the state. I had read about the new "open classrooms" which were being built in other areas. Each pod contained four classrooms and could also be used as one giant classroom. I think the architect had already planned the "open classroom" as a money-saving idea.

The day before school was out, I gave Hank my answer. I would be the last principal in Jerome and the first one in the high school in Cottonwood. Talk about selling out for an open auditorium!

At our end-of-school party, it became known among the staff I would be their next principal. They all wished me well even though they subtly warned me I wouldn't like it. In some cases, it wasn't subtle at all.

By the way, at that time, I didn't have an administrator's certification. I faced spending the summer again at NAU to become certified. Meanwhile I fought hard to get the things I wanted for the "new Mingus High." I enjoyed those summer sessions at the university because Dr. Louie MacDonald was one of my instructors. I also enjoyed dreaming about things in our new school which we wanted but didn't have in Jerome.

> "Don't lose sight of good planning and insight. Hang onto them, for they fill you with life and bring you honor and respect," Proverbs 3:21-22.

Chapter 14

To lean a bit on Charles Dickens' great opening lines of his novel, *Tale of Two Cities,* I became an administrator during the "best of times and the worst of times." Certainly the best part was being in meetings when the board, teachers, and architect were planning the new school. As the school principal, people gave me more of a listen than they, perhaps, would have if I were still a teacher.

Some things I fought for did not figure in the minds of persons who held more traditional views of what a school should be. Hard wooden floors were the norm before, but I held out for carpeting. It would be much quieter than the halls of the Jerome school were. I was cautioned to call carpeting "acoustical floor covering" rather than just carpeting. That name, of course, sounded much more practical and less frilly and expensive than carpeting would be.

Having experienced the lockers in the halls of Jerome, I wanted self-locking doors on them instead of key or combination locks. I also wanted the lockers to have a slanting top to prevent students from piling books and papers on top as they did in Jerome. "It would be nice also if lockers could be colorfully painted so they could enhance the beauty of the place," I remarked. I won that battle. They were very colorful and nice looking when they were installed.

Bob Starkovich recommended the library be open to the halls. "It works beautifully in Tempe's new city hall and library."

I disagreed saying if it were open, students in the halls would bother those in the library by throwing papers, etc. "Adults use the city hall library in Tempe while it's mostly kids here." Bob agreed, and the library had a view of the halls, but only through window glass.

My main concern was to have an auditorium open all the time. Critics of this pointed out acoustics would be difficult in such a place, and people in the halls could bother those trying to perform on the stage. Bob answered this by suggesting "acoustical clouds" near the ceiling which would carry sound to the 900 seats.

In meetings about the building, any suggestion was always met with objections, but Starkovich began to battle on the side of openness, and we scraped by. Theater-type seating also met with opposition because of the expense, but we also won the battle since our auditorium would be used by the whole Verde Valley. Hank Barbarick fought hard for the beautiful open auditorium as I did, and it has served all the communities well. A Sedonan even donated a beautiful Grand piano to help solidify the community/school idea.

I know most teachers never have the opportunity I had to help fashion a school since they most often work in a place which is already built. Teachers should always have a list of suggestions to make when they have a chance during any remodeling. In our case, teachers were constantly asked to bring their ideas to the table.

While I got some of my ideas into the new school, becoming principal then was also the worst of times. These were the years of student rebellion on college campuses, and some rebelling filtered down to the high schools. The war in Vietnam was raging and much of the country was divided. Because of the division, there were many more issues than now. Dress codes were strictly enforced, and it became one of the major jobs of the principal to enforce those dress codes. Then it was "fashionable" for girls to wear skirts as short as possible. Students were often tricky about this. The girls would leave home with what the parents and school considered respectable skirt lengths, but they would roll up the waist to make the skirt shorter when they arrived at school. When parents were called in to confer about the violation of the code, the kids would roll the skirt down to proper length making me appear to be a bit of a liar. Fortunately most of the parents knew about the tricks and sympathized with me.

The length of boys' hair was also an issue. The school board wanted no long-haired boys in the school. Long hair was part of the protesting about the war. One of the first students I talked with on this issue left school and took us to court. The ACLU backed the boy, and we were summoned to court. We won the case—one of the few schools that did—but the boy chose to remain out of school. He was a very intelligent, nice boy who would have been a credit to our school.

Drugs also became an issue. While I was almost ambivalent on the dress and hair codes, I wasn't when it came to illegal drugs. The teachers and I all worked together attempting to keep our students "drug free." I know the struggle still rages in our society today.

I scheduled myself for an early-bird class in the English curriculum. Jim MacLarney and I had worked out an English program which was a bit different from traditional schools. We sent letters to many schools in Arizona and California requesting copies of their English curricula and we became "idea thieves."

We decided each of our classes should only be semester courses. This gave students some choices about their study of writing and literature. We had one-semester, specialized courses in Poetry, Science Fiction, American Literature, English Literature, and World Literature. Writing and grammar were to be part of each course. Our small student body reacted favorably to this—in fact, it was so successful other schools, including Mr. West's Kingman school, asked us to explain our program to them. I was invited to give an "in-service" workshop to the Kingman schools. We named our program, "The Scope and Sequence of the English Department." We were pleased when we heard some other schools adopted our plan.

We had a textbook called *Philosophy of Literature* for high schools. I chose it to teach many of our better students who enrolled in the class in their senior year. It was fun to teach the elements of fiction to willing students as we saw those elements in the stories and poems we read.

Perhaps it was the title *Philosophy of Literature* which drew many of the most-advanced students to the early-bird class. The book was a brilliant collection of classic stories and poems which were challenging but interesting. Included were things I only experienced in college.

After a few classes, I decided to try something a bit different. I gave groups of three or four students a story or poem to explain to the whole class, and they were to be prepared to answer any questions about it. I gave them several days to read and discuss their assignment with each other. Then I had them go to the center of a half-circle of student desks to talk about the story. They worked on their assignment diligently. It was a total success.

I had a student teacher from NAU then. She was very intelligent and hardworking. However, one day I left her alone for some reason and went to the office. After class, she came in crying, "These students are so wonderful I'm afraid I can never be a teacher. Most of them are ahead of me." I assured her she would be a good teacher, and she was. She taught at the middle school and told me my method worked on her level as well. One of these students came back and told me she was put on television in Chicago because only she and another student knew much about the elements of fiction in her college freshman class. I loved compliments like that. Sometimes they are even better than payday.

Again here is another bit of philosophy from one who had experience as teacher, principal, and board member. I urge every administrator to teach at least one class a year. I firmly believe administrators who teach don't often lose sight of what goes on in "the trenches."

The majority of school budgets should go to the classrooms as well. As sole principal, I was paid only $500 more than was paid to the highest paid teacher in the school. I disagree wholeheartedly with the notion school administrators' salaries should be much higher than those of the teachers. Again, I realize administrators face awesome responsibilities and often are called to serve more hours than teachers.

Aside from some of the difficult issues, I had some fun as principal in Jerome. One day after the lunch period was over, Mrs. Franklin, our secretary, came into my office saying, "There are two girls out there you need to see immediately." She was extremely agitated.

After showing the crying girls in, she closed the door—which was hardly ever closed.

"She got raped while going to music class!" blurted out one of the girls while pointing to the other one who sat there sobbing.

Needless to say, that got my full attention. I went out to the secretary and asked for a box of tissues. When I returned, I handed each girl some of the tissues and asked them to calm down and tell me exactly what had happened.

"Well, we were upstairs going to music class when he jumped out and raped her. It was terrible!"

If I were sweating before, it was mild to the sweat now generated by my fears. I pointed to the sobbing "raped girl" and asked her what happened exactly. She was too busy crying to give me a rational answer, but her companion spoke up again. "He (naming the student) came out from the pile of wrestling mats and kissed her."

"And then . . ." I asked, "What happened then?" I was very afraid of what her answer would be.

"That's all. She didn't want him to kiss her. That's rape, isn't it?"

Breathing a sigh of relief, I asked, "Has he tried to kiss you before?"

The sobbing girl spoke for the first time. "Yes, and I told him that I didn't like him. He keeps bothering me."

"Girls, you need to find out what rape means. His trying to kiss you probably happened because he likes you. Would it be okay with you if I called him in and ordered him to leave you alone?"

"I guess," they both said, "but when someone tries to kiss you, but you don't want him to, isn't it rape?"

"No, it isn't rape. Rape is much worse than that." After a short talk about rape, I accompanied them back to their classroom. They were obviously feeling better because they both laughed a bit while we walked.

Then I called for the boy. When he came in, he was also crying. "I scared her, Mr. Gabrielson. I love her. I have loved her since we were in grade school together. I promise that I won't do it again. Please don't call my parents."

"I think if you apologize to her, it will go a long way to soothe bad feelings. Come with me."

We went to the music class and called the girls out. The boy apologized very sincerely. He told her he would leave her alone, but he loved her.

She accepted his apology, and they shook on it.

When I told Hank about this, I thought he'd fall off his chair laughing. "Welcome to the club, Ernie."

The real problem we had was no laughing matter. We couldn't sell the bonds since the market was not conducive for institutions to loan money. We continued in our old school hoping someone would loan us the money we bonded for. We, the faculty, were so anxious we even considered a suggestion we borrow the money ourselves and buy the bonds. That idea, while ridiculous, arose because we were so desperate.

> "Looking for the solution without listening to the problem is working in the dark," Unknown.

Chapter 15

It was a worrisome time while we waited for someone to buy the bonds. Merle Crawford discussed writing to members of Congress, the State Legislature, and other political groups. While we talked about how we could help, we really didn't have a clue. Weeks and months went by until one day Hank announced the First National Bank had purchased the bonds. We really celebrated after hearing that.

Soon after, the plans of the new school were finished, and we waited for construction to begin. Hank and I discussed the feasibility of taking the entire student body down to the site to watch the ground-breaking ceremony. We decided everyone could be transported if students doubled up on the buses. When we arrived at the site, we saw many officials of Cottonwood, school board members, newspaper reporters, photographers, and even just some curious citizens of the Verde Valley. A giant cheer went up from the student body when several officials, including Hank, took a "golden" shovelful of dirt and then posed for pictures. After that, I was given the microphone and attempted to show the students where the various rooms would be located. I may not have been even close to accurate, but it was fun to get them imagining the completed building. We all knew construction would take many months, but one could sense the excitement not only in the students but in the entire valley. Every time Bob Starkovich came up to school he discussed with specific teachers what they wanted in the classrooms. Of course, many wanted things that would take too much money so they had to wait and hold onto their dreams. Many people associated with the school made almost daily trips to the site as the ground was being prepared.

One day Carroll and I went to Phoenix for something. After dinner and as dusk fell, we left for home. About 50 miles from Phoenix, we spotted two trucks with long flat trailers struggling up the hill above Black Canyon City. They each carried many steel beams, and I said to Carroll, "I think those are for our new high school." I was right. The next morning almost before dawn, I went to the site, and there were the beams along with dozens of construction workers. The new school was finally begun.

Every time I went up to check on progress, I met many of the staff and students also "checking." Meanwhile, school went on in Jerome. During the late winter of 1971 and early in 1972, the new school began to look like a school. At the end of the school year, it was debated where the Class of '72 would graduate. We wanted it to be in the new auditorium, but the seats were not in place yet. We decided they would like being the first to graduate in their new school, so we had the gym bleachers ready for parents and friends while the graduates and speakers were in chairs on the new gym floor, which was covered with sheets of heavy paper. That ceremony signaled the end of classes graduating on the football field in Clarkdale where we had to sweat out the weather.

During the spring and summer of '72, I had the most fun I ever had as principal. As the finishing touches were being made, many students came asking for a tour. I was happy to walk around with them as they explored their wonderful school. On one of the tours, a student said to me, "Don't worry about vandalism, Mr. Gabrielson. We'll make sure no one will dare do something bad here. All of us who came from the old school will watch out for freshmen who might not appreciate how wonderful this is."

I loved their excitement and joy as they walked around. They walked through the pods that would house four classes with no walls to separate them one from the other. None of the students had ever heard of this "open classroom" type of learning, but they enjoyed thinking about it.

The school, of course, was not nearly finished, but we moved in during the fall of 1972. The parking lots were just scraped off vacant land—no paving yet. There was no football stadium, no softball or baseball fields, no tennis courts, etc. Those things had to come later as more money became available.

In spite of not having some things which would come later, all of us were very excited on the first day of school. All the students were seated in the auditorium, and I was proud to be the one who welcomed them. I watched as students wandered around the halls, and I was pleased about how quiet it was.

I'm also very proud when years later Tom Henry called me the "Father of Mingus Union" because I had twisted a few arms when elected president of the *association*, so I could encourage the board to at least try passing a bond issue to build our school in Cottonwood. Since opening day in '72, the student body has grown to well over a thousand, and additional buildings have been built along with many "playing fields." During the following years, Hank Barbarick, the staff and board, and I worked hard for many of the things Mingus Union has today.

I loved Mingus High School during all my years there and I still do. I wrote this letter to the editor of the *Verde Independent* urging the passage of a $15 million bond issue in 2007. After the election, the board president sent me a letter informing me my letter was a big reason for the successful passage.

Editor:
Mingus Union High School left Jerome in 1972 trailing clouds of glory and splendid traditions. As

principal of the school then, I shared in the pride our students, faculty, and community had in our beautiful new facility. I know that it became a model for schools throughout the state and nation.

During the nearly 40 years that have passed since, Mingus Union entered the hearts and lives of thousands of students and community members who are proud to have been part of it.

Now this glorious school needs a bit of help. I'm very frustrated that I can't vote "yes" in November to help her, but I hope that she, as well as the whole lovely Verde Valley will hear my prayers for success in the bond election—even though those prayers are from far away Tucson.

I know that one can't really love brick and mortar, but I shall always love the spirit of Mingus Union. Please give her the help she needs on Nov. 7.

"The Difficult is that which can be done immediately; The impossible is that which takes a little longer." George Santayana

Chapter 16

After the new school opened, we realized some of the "frills" were not only wanted but were needed. The fall of '72 was one of the wettest I can remember. Every day the students parked on a muddy lot and tramped mud into the halls and classrooms.

Most of the teachers disliked the open pods because one could hear and see into the other classrooms. Portable sliding vinyl walls were added later to allow for privacy while keeping the option of shared classrooms.

In front of the building on Fir Street, it looked like a building was built on part of a vacant lot. In short, our beautiful new school was not beautifully landscaped.

During my seven years as principal, I made many mistakes and had many bad days; however, I loved many of those days in spite of problems caused by a shortage of funds.

During the second or third year of the new school, I received a form letter from Governor Williams urging all Arizona schools to plant a tree on Arbor Day. When I read the letter, I took it into the superintendent's office and asked Hank, "Do we have any money for something like this?"

"Ernie," he replied, "I'm trying to scrape up enough to get some needed furniture. The trees will have to wait."

I went back into my office and angrily threw the letter into the wastebasket. As I sat there, I had an idea. I called the Student Council into my office. They were seated in extra chairs I brought in. After I thanked them for coming, I read the Governor's letter and I wrote a check for $50. Then I asked them if they'd like to see some trees and shrubs planted around the building. "Can you folks pass the hat around to the other students to see if we can raise enough to have a wonderful Arbor Day? I hope this check starts a good fund." *Privately I wondered how I would explain the check to Carroll when I got home.*

All of them became enthusiastic about the idea and began to chatter about how best to do this. As I listened, they came up with the idea of going to specific classrooms every day during the third period class. I said I would go to all the service clubs asking them for donations. The council members tore out of my office like a fired-up football team.

Every day the students brought in money from the student body, and I was successful with the service organizations. In a week, we had collected over $3,000. I knew it was enough to require an expert to come up with a great landscaping plan. I went to Carlton Camp, the agricultural representative from the University of Arizona. He told me the project was too big for him, but he called a friend who was a landscape expert in Phoenix and asked him to come and work with us. He came, and together we walked around as he sketched a rough map. He said his work would be free to us if we allowed him to bring half of our plants up from his nursery in Phoenix. "The other half should come from local nurseries. I will see to all purchases, and I'll get the best deal possible," he said.

Steve Dockery, the Vocational Agriculture teacher, spent the next days having his students dig holes in very hard claiche where the new trees and plants would go. The day before Arbor Day, I announced, "Students who come with a shovel and work clothes will be excused from classes." To be quite honest, I didn't know there were so many shovels in the whole valley. The fertilizer and trees were planted according to the landscape plan. It was a great day. We planted 234 trees, plants and shrubs. During the day, I wandered around. Once I spotted several students gathered around a hole. I went over to one girl saying, "Come on. You were excused to work, not just sit and talk."

She showed me her hand which was covered with a big blister and said, "Mr. Gabrielson, I have been working." She made me feel like a small insect as I apologized to her and slithered away.

During the weekend, I received several phone calls from students volunteering to come to water the new plants. I was very proud of our students during the whole planting campaign.

In the years following, I never saw anyone do anything to harm our work on that fabulous Arbor Day. There was much more to be done, but it was a great start. When someone talks despairingly about "kids today," I can't agree. I wish they knew about our wonderful kids. They raised the money, planted the trees, and worked until blistered to make their school beautiful. I think, perhaps, there is a lesson here. Kids will be proud of their campuses and schools if they are allowed to be part of them.

During the next fall, Hank said he was having the front area leveled for grass which was always a dream of mine. There would be underground pipes to water this large area. After the grass was planted, he came into my office concerned, "Ernie, you need to put some signs up telling the students to stay off the grass."

"I don't think that's necessary, Hank. They won't harm it because they want it to grow beautiful just as much as we do."

"I think that's a mistake, Ernie. Let's see." He returned to his office then. The grass grew well, and during most seasons, the front lawn is one of the most beautiful in the Verde Valley. Finally the parking lot was paved and lighted so mud was no longer a problem.

Our tennis teams had to play and practice on the courts in Sedona which were about 20 miles away. I wanted courts on campus. A girl named Sandra Goss was the state singles champion in spite of us not having proper courts. Hank, again, came through with some funds we got from another bond election. We built several courts and fenced them. I remember the difficulty of digging holes for the fence posts. The ground was so hard it bent shovels as we tried to dig holes. I sent one of the custodians down to rent a jack hammer. As he was working it through the ground, a student said, "That looks like fun." I knew from working in the mines in Bisbee handling a jack hammer was no fun, but I asked him if he'd like to try. He said, "Would I?" He took it and started working. He lasted about 20 seconds. It was actually longer than I thought he would last.

On the day the courts were finished and fenced, the foreman of the construction crew brought me the key to the lock on the gate. "All finished," he said.

I went out and unlocked the gate and gave the key to Mrs. Franklin with the instruction, "Hide this key, Georgia. Don't tell anyone where it is—not even me."

A couple of hours later, Hank came with his usual concern. "We should lock the courts when they're not in use."

"I don't think so, Hank. Remember this is a community school. We sold the first bond issue by promising that. Let's try it open, so the community can use it when we're not."

Since then, the tennis courts have been added to, and a football stadium and softball and baseball diamonds have been built. I'm very proud I had something to do with initiating the start of our campus, but I'm prouder still that our student body was so active and enthusiastic about it.

Another little note: When Sandra Goss was a senior playing in the state tennis tournament, one school said they had no boy tennis team, so they let a boy play on the girls' team. I was irate about it and tried to have him disqualified from the girls' tournament, but I was not successful. I told Miss LeVering if Sandra had to play the boy, it would be okay with me if she forfeited the match and walked away lodging a protest. Sandra again won the championship for the fourth time and defeated the boy along the way. She trounced him!

> "The difference between an unsuccessful person and others is not a lack of strength, not a lack of knowledge, but rather a lack of will," Vince Lombardi

Chapter 17

My seven years as principal is not a time I remember too fondly. There were things I had to do every day which I hated doing. Telling a student sitting across from my desk his grades made him ineligible for team sports was almost as painful for me as it was for him. And, again, for one reason or another, I had to have conferences with teachers concerning a problem they were having in class. Parents and grandparents often questioned my decisions concerning the disciplining of their loved one. One parent even said I ruined her son's life when I suspended him from the football team when he was arrested for drunkenness. It seemed to me every day brought forth a new crisis. Also as principal, I was expected to be there whenever there was any kind of activity or game. This, of course, interfered with my family life as my two kids were growing up.

A couple of years after I retired, my son was in "sports radio" in Tucson. He sent me a tape which he made of his Father's Day program. I loved it because he said, "Often when Dad came home after a bad day as principal, he still had time to forget his problems and do things with us kids. Even when he was dog tired, he came out to the back yard and played catch with me, and he always had time to read us stories before we went to bed."

Not being able to spend as much time with my kids as I wanted was one of the chief reasons I resigned as principal and went back to teaching.

Once I said a day without being threatened with a lawsuit was as rare as a cold day in summer.

Twice, I was put in the very uncomfortable position of firing teachers. One time occurred after warning a teacher who made a practice of being absent for "illness" too often. While the school board granted unlimited sick leave, abusing it was not kosher to me and to others who work every day. No substitute, regardless of ability, can work with a class as well as a regular teacher.

Sadly, I had to also fire a teacher for "unprofessional conduct" with a student. He was fired on the spot, and I had to get a substitute to finish the year. However, the superintendent and board always backed up these tough decisions.

I also had to interview prospective teaching candidates. I look back with a smile on interviewing a candidate for music instructor. A lovely young lady just out of college came to Cottonwood seeking employment as the music teacher. Her papers were top-notch, and she was very charming. She indicated she and her fiancé came up from Phoenix for her interview. After she said he was also a recent graduate seeking a teaching position, I asked her to invite him in. When he came into my office, he said he was a history major with a minor in German. At the time, we needed a history teacher, and I thought we probably should offer German as a foreign language as well as Spanish and French. Because there was no immediate need to hire a music teacher, the girl did not get the job, but her fiancé did. The girl eventually got a job in Cottonwood and finally came to Mingus as an outstanding teacher. Her husband, Dave, also an outstanding teacher, retired from Mingus after many years of service.

When basketball coach Tom Henry wanted to quit basketball and go back to just classroom teaching, we advertised for a basketball coach. One day a very small fellow came to interview for that position. Right off the bat, I felt he couldn't have played much basketball with his short stature; but his resumé stated he had played on UCLA's great teams under legendary coach Wooten. His credentials appeared to be excellent, but I had to question his claim to have played on UCLA's national championship teams. However, I took him down to Tom Henry and introduced him. After he left, Tom said he was skeptical of his claim. I took the problem to

Superintendent Barbarick who said, "Call UCLA, Ernie, and find out." Coach Wooten was not available because he was recruiting and wouldn't be back for several days.

Each day, the candidate showed up almost pleading with me for the job. One day he came down from Jerome with a friend. The man from Jerome, a restaurant owner, told me the young man wanted the job so bad he had lied on his resumé, but I should hire him anyway. Of course, it was not to be, and I made an enemy of the man from Jerome who apparently thought his knowing me would be enough to convince me to hire the young man. Unfortunately forged credentials have allowed many rascals into teaching positions. Every candidate's credentials should be checked for false statements and forged letters of recommendation.

Once one of our physical education teachers, Harriet LeVering, caught a member of her team with a bottle of liquor on the bus when they were returning from Phoenix. I suspended the girl for a five-day period and told her she was permanently suspended from the team. The next morning, her father came to my office roaring mad. "If you suspended my daughter, you should also suspend the teacher."

"Why would I suspend the teacher? For doing her job?"

Not being mollified, he threatened to have the superintendent and board fire me. He did go to Hank and the board but got nowhere. I believe he thought his daughter never did anything wrong and I never did anything right.

Once I got a survey form from the Department of Education in Washington. The letter with it stated Mingus had been one of few schools in the country singled out for a "surname survey." They wanted me to go through the names of all our students and identify them as to whether they were Asian, Native American, Latin, or Anglo Saxon. Since I didn't believe in this kind of separation of our kids, I didn't fill out the form. Days later I received a call from a person at the Department of Education. A very officious voice asked me why I hadn't sent the completed survey back. I told him I didn't believe in it, since no real reason was included with the letter.

"Just a minute! You have to talk to my superior," he threatened. Not holding his hand tightly enough over his phone, I heard him say, "Just some Podunk school out in Arizona."

Another officious voice came on and told me this was government business, and I needed to send the information back right away. His voice and attitude indicated he thought bullying tactics would get the result he wanted since he was sure I was sufficiently intimidated by the privilege of talking to a supervisor in the Department of Education.

"As principal of a Podunk high school in Arizona, let me ask you, Sir: Have you read the United States Constitution lately? Education is the responsibility of the states—not the national government. If the state asks me to, I'll send the damn form, but let me tell you this is not just a Podunk school."

After I hung up, I told Mr. Barbarick what had happened. He smiled, and said, "I'll bet we get a call from the State Department within a half hour."

He was wrong on the time. It took less than 10 minutes to get the call from Phoenix. "Send 'em the damn form, please." We both laughed, as I said I would. I'll remember that phone call for the rest of my life because I enjoyed it so much.

Schools across the nation are now losing control because the Federal government gains more control each year. While I laughed about that call, we can see the states are losing more and more control to the Federal government regardless of the intent of our Constitution.

Once when I was standing in the auditorium near the office, a man came to me and asked, "Can you direct me to the principal's office?"

I told him I was the principal and asked him what I could do for him.

"You aren't dressed like a principal," he said with a smile. "Most of them wear a necktie." He was dressed in a nice-looking coat with a neck tie and was carrying a brief case. "This is a new school, and I'd like to be shown around. I'm looking at a number of new schools in the West." I took him around the plant and showed him the buildings as they were, and I also shared with him my dreams of what it would be when it acquired a few "frills." Later I got a nice thank-you letter from him. He was from Washington with a department which evaluated construction, and we were told later his department indicated Mingus Union probably got more for their dollars than any other school in the country. I loved hearing that.

One day in the spring, I went into the superintendent's office and asked to resign at the end of the year and go back to teaching full time.

"Ernie, what if I give you an assistant? Will you stay?"

"No, Hank. I want to teach."

"You won't like going back—grading papers and all."

"Hank, we've gone through two bond elections. We've got a nice school now, and things are going smoothly. I want to spend the rest of my career in the classroom."

I was proud of the fact each member of the school board and some of our faculty along with many people in the community asked me to stay. Sitting behind an administrator's desk was not how I wanted to spend the rest of my career. I wanted to teach!

> "The trouble with being a leader today is that you can't be sure whether people are following you or chasing you," Anonymous.

Chapter 18

After I resigned as principal, I continued serving until the fall semester started. I worked hard to have everything in order for my successor, but the light at the end of the tunnel was getting very bright. I almost hungered to get back into the classroom fulltime even though I already was teaching an early-bird class in Speed Reading. Also I often "substituted" when teachers had to miss classes because of some other commitment.

Ruth Wicks, one of our counselors, asked me to take her history class the next day because she had to attend a conference. "We're not reading the book because it's too hard for most of the class. Can you teach them about the <u>Declaration of Independence</u>—that's the lesson for tomorrow?"

"Don't worry, Ruth. I can handle it." In fact, I was looking forward to it. I thought back to my history teacher in high school who assigned everyone a book to report on. My book was *Oliver Wiswell*, an historical novel written by Kenneth Roberts. He wrote many novels about the Revolutionary War. Mine, however, was about a fellow who became a Tory and fought to stay loyal to Britain and stood firmly against Independence. When I finished reading it, I began to see there were two legitimate sides in the American Colonies. I had fought against thinking we might not be 100% right in our understanding of the struggle. That book opened my mind a bit because I started to see both sides.

When I walked into Miss Wicks' class the next day, I opened with a question. "How many of you have read the <u>Declaration of Independence</u>?" With that question, I discovered only one or two had even glanced at it.

"If you were a member of the Continental Congress at that time, would you have signed it? Raise your hands if you would."

Of course, everyone who was paying the slightest bit of attention raised their hands. *I smiled inwardly because they just indicated they would sign a contract before reading it.*

"Why?" I asked, 'is the <u>Declaration</u> an important and famous document?"

"Because it made us a nation," responded a good student from Sedona. "My dad said it's very important in our history."

I looked at him with a smile and said, "The first few paragraphs are very beautiful, Mr. Jefferson, but are they true?"

"They are," the young man said. "Why would it be so famous, if it wasn't true?" He looked at me as if I had lost my marbles for even suggesting those words might not be true—after all we still celebrated its signing.

"Mr. Jefferson, there is a famous man in England named Samuel Johnson who said, 'I could support the American cause if it weren't for the fact one-sixth of their population are slaves.' Now, Mr. Jefferson, can you explain the phrase you use, 'all men are created equal' as one of the self-evident truths in spite of what Mr. Johnson said?"

The boy began to sputter, and everyone in the class was now paying some attention to our small debate.

"Is it true, Mr. Jefferson, that you yourself own slaves? Isn't what you said a little hypocritical? And, Sir, you say 'all men.' What about women? Are they not equal?"

"But only traitors won't sign the <u>Declaration of Independence</u>. All the true patriots signed it, didn't they?" The boy asked this question even though he was not sure he would get the answer he wanted.

"Tom, the people on the other side were called *Loyalists*. Can you define loyalist?"

"Well, isn't it a person who stays loyal?"

"You're right, Mr. Jefferson. Now tell me how many of the delegates here in Congress are black or women? Certainly there are a number of blacks and women in the colonies. Are they created equal?"

The class began to laugh at "Mr. Jefferson" as he tried to find answers to my questions.

"Tom, the blacks won't become free and enjoy the blessings of liberty until the Civil War, and women won't be allowed to vote in national elections until 1920. Do you all believe you would have signed the document?" There were a few hands raised now, but tentatively. I knew they were now thinking. *Maybe now they'd at least read a contract before signing it.*

"Now let's all turn to the <u>Declaration</u> in the back of your book." They all opened the text to find it. "Now, Mr. Jefferson, would you read those first two paragraphs out loud as we follow along?"

After he had read them, I said, "Tom Jefferson outlined in those wonderful words what America was to stand for after independence was achieved. Those paragraphs have become America's beacon. They are wonderfully beautiful, and the whole world now admires them. They are well-worth memorizing." I then quoted those paragraphs word-for-word with a bit of drama trying to convince them I had done what I asked them to do.

I walked over to the student who played Jefferson so well and said, "I hope maybe this class opened the minds of everyone in it a little today, and <u>you</u> helped. Thank you for helping me do this lesson." I shook his hand while receiving a great smile. "Thanks for standing up for what you believe. Now, class, let me tell a story I read once." I think all of them were listening.

"In 1940, at the beginning of the Second World War, the German army had conquered most of Western Europe. Hitler's army was entering the Netherlands. The Nazi forces were occupying large and small towns in Holland. A small-town high school teacher was informed the Nazi soldiers would be in town the next day, so the teacher knew he was teaching his last lesson. He chose to have his students memorize these first two or three paragraphs which Tom Jefferson wrote way back in 1776. I believe he couldn't have chosen a better *last lesson*. What do you think, class?" Most of them turned to their books and began to memorize. It seemed as though all of them caught the "spirit of 1776."

I went back to the desk and said, "The lesson here is to look at both sides before you jump to a conclusion." I gave them the rest of the period to memorize those first paragraphs. I believe most of them did memorize them.

After her history class the next day, Miss Wicks said, "The kids were really wound up about the Declaration of Independence. They said you asked them some good questions which made them think."

I hope I did. One of my teaching mottos is by Albert Einstein. He once said, "The aim of education is not to fill the mind, but to open it." I hope all teachers believe this. It's a lot of fun to see the minds of students begin to open. In ancient Athens, Socrates taught people to think by asking questions which opened minds. We, as teachers, need to do the same. To see a bit of confusion in their faces is a treat. Confusion comes first as the thinking process begins.

A teacher once wrote that teachers should use about 28 interrogatory sentences for each declarative one.

Playing the "Devil's Advocate" is a fun way to start class discussions. It opened the minds of the ancient Greeks when Socrates did it, and it works when today's classroom teachers do it.

> "The wrong way to teach history would be to show that there's only one perspective and only one history,"
> Jonathan Wenn

Chapter 19

On the day before fall semester was to begin, we invited Mr. and Mrs. Toms (the new principal and his wife) to dinner. In the morning, I took my last tour around the building to show him where doors needed to be unlocked and lights turned on. Then I gave him my keys and went into the faculty room. I felt like I had just returned home after a long absence. I knew that room would never be as wild and rowdy as the one in Jerome, but it felt good to be there nevertheless. I was also concerned about how the faculty would welcome me back from my years as an administrator. I was pleasantly surprised when they all welcomed me as if I had never left their ranks. That did a lot for my morale.

I believe I had three junior English classes and two sophomore classes. I still had the early-bird Speed Reading course.

While I was getting my administrator certificate, I also was taking classes which would give me an EDS degree. That degree is one between the masters and the doctorate. In obtaining it, I became a certified reading specialist. I whole-heartedly think since reading is the basis of most learning, efficient reading should be something all teachers should learn and teach. A good method is an old reading tool—SQ3R (survey, question, read, review and recite). In many cases, a simple survey of the material is all that's needed. It is simply scanning through the material to find the main ideas.

I always loved teaching "speed reading" because I knew its future value to students, and I never really had to work hard to sell its value to them. When they became juniors and seniors, most were already highly motivated to go to higher education.

On the first day of class, I explained the course was really "efficient reading." I explained efficient reading is covering the material well in the shortest possible time.

"The first thing we need to consider is getting rid of bad reading habits." We talked about how hard it is to break long-held habits. As a fun thing, I sent them out of class to do things they didn't always do—things like putting on shoes and clothes differently. "Tonight, don't sit in the chair you normally sit in. Handle silverware differently. In short, try to see how habits are part of your life and often control you."

The next day, we talked about some of their experiences trying to break ingrained habits. I explained how a hypothetical student studies for an exam.

> "He comes home carrying his book with good intentions, but puts off studying until he watches *his program* on TV and puts it off again until after dinner. He excuses himself to go to his bedroom <u>where he can study in quiet</u>. But first, he must phone his friend talking for about 30 minutes while the opened book sits there. Then he starts day-dreaming about a girl whom he's taking to the after-game dance on Friday. He receives a phone call from another friend and then after looking at his watch rationalizes he can pass the test by reading the rest of the chapter on the bus going to school. He only glances at a paragraph while the bus is in motion amid the noise of laughter and conversation. The book remains closed as he thinks he studied for two hours the night before."

The kids laughed about that student and admitted it was the truth.

Once I had a mother call me to inquire why her son got an F for the grading period. "What color is his history book?" I asked her.

"I er . . . I really don't know." After a pause, she said, "I see what you mean. I'll make sure I know what it looks like tonight."

"What are some of our bad reading habits?" a student asked.

I explained lack of concentration is perhaps the worst. Reading everything at the same rate of speed is another. "For example, let's take a trip to Phoenix from Cottonwood (about 100 miles) Hopping into an airplane, the trip would take less than a half hour. You'll get there, but you won't see much of the scenery. A car trip takes about two hours, but you can see some countryside as you zip by. On horseback or on a bike you can see more scenery, but it takes a day or two. Walking takes about three or four days, but you really can smell the flowers on the trip. We must set our reading speed considering our purpose and the difficulty of the material. We should read novels at one speed, but poetry is read at a much slower pace savoring the beauty of the words.

Another bad habit is being easily distracted by noise."

"But I know lots of good students who read and study while listening to music," a student spoke up a little defensively.

I replied, "Music is okay only if you don't actively listen. If it's only in the background, music is okay but not if you are really "listening" to it. Most of us can only do <u>one</u> thing well at a time. Always bring your imagination with you when you read. See in your mind's eye what the author is describing. After you have it in your mind, you can skip most of his descriptive words. That's the advantage of reading and listening over movies and TV. They both tend to rob us of using our own imaginations."

We had many timed drills until I knew they were concentrating hard in order to finish the material in the allotted time. Often they raced hoping to beat their own speed established the day before. They found studying a chapter of a book was easy if they first "surveyed" the material rapidly to find the general idea. Then they tried to form questions in their minds about what they wanted from it. Then they read it—not word by word but idea by idea.

I enjoyed watching them read while I dropped things, opened doors and noisily re-arranged some furniture while watching them read without looking up. By the end of the course, they all knew concentration is the most important thing in reading and studying. I had reports from them that they took much less time to study for tests than previously and did much better on them.

Many students told me their grades improved significantly after taking "Speed Reading." I was very pleased when a brilliant boy came back after a year at Stanford University. He said, "Mr. Gabrielson, I would never have passed the first semester at Stanford, but for the Speed Reading course." A comment like that is music to a teacher's ears.

All teachers need to be aware of techniques to foster better reading and study habits regardless of the subject. They must always keep in mind pupils are in school to <u>learn how to learn</u>. Good study habits will serve a student well for a life time.

"There's not a nickel's worth of difference between those who can't read and those who can but don't," Mark Twain.

Chapter 20

When the newest building opened, I was assigned a room there.

I soon found out the faculty was still a close-knit group. Sometimes the spirit we had in the smaller school became true in the bigger, more-sophisticated one. One day I was sitting in the very small faculty room in the new building. Space there was limited, but we made do. The room was tiny compared with the main building's spacious faculty room. It was merely a counter with several chairs pushed under it.

Our new drama/English teacher, Vaughn Hatch, Bob Cox (another English teacher) and I were just sitting in there shooting the bull one day. However it happened, we began talking about a beloved school bus driver and custodian named Lupe Uribe.

I told them a story about how much Lupe treasured his hitch in the Marine Corps. There was little doubt he loved the

Corps because he told me he often went into the main office to play a recording of the Marine Hymn over the loud speakers to listen to while cleaning classrooms during the night shift.

"Hey, it's the first of November. The Marine birthday is November 10th, only a few days away," Cox said. "Maybe we should do something special for Lupe."

I fell in with the plan, as did the drama teacher. The stage was set for working out the details. We decided the kids would like it if we had a "Lupe Uribe Day" at Mingus, and the birthday of the Corps would be perfect.

Bob said, "I read somewhere Ed McMahon of the <u>Johnnie Carson Show</u> regularly sends telegrams to old Marines on special occasions. I'll try to contact him, and perhaps he'll send one honoring Lupe."

Vaughn said while looking at me, "I'll work up a small announcement if you can convince Hank that we want to talk about Lupe and the Marines just before the daily announcements."

"I don't think it'll be hard because Hank and Lupe get along. In addition, I'll contact the Marine recruiting office in Phoenix to see if they have any suggestions and if they might like to participate." Now we had a full-blown plan, but that's always scary since plans sometimes blow sky high. A few days later, Bob said he had received a congratulatory telegram from Ed McMahon addressed to Lupe congratulating him on "his special day." McMahon had been a colonel while in the Marines. A few days before Nov. 10, the Marine office in Phoenix contacted me saying they would be happy to take part in the ceremony.

Early in the morning on November 10, two Marines came to the office dressed in their dress blues and carrying a large and beautiful wall hanging of the Marine emblem.

Hank participated by sending Lupe down into the custodian's room and told another custodian to bring him up when the announcement went over the air. Fortunately, it was my free period and I, along with the Marines, stood in the office doorway overlooking the auditorium while Vaughn read the special message we had written. I can't remember the exact words, but this is the essence:

"Today is November 10. This is the 202nd birthday of the United States Marine Corps. The Corps was established on this date in 1775 at Tun's Tavern in Philadelphia. Today, the Marines wish to honor one of their own. Today, we want the entire faculty and student body to help us celebrate "Lupe Uribe Day." Would Lupe come now to the office to receive a gift from the Marine Corps recruiting office in Phoenix?" Then Vaughn Hatch read the telegram from Ed McMahon.

The students poured out of the classrooms bordering the auditorium, and others came to witness the scene as Lupe came to the office. There was spontaneous applauding as Lupe came forward. When he saw the Marines standing there with the beautiful emblem and listened to McMahon's telegram over the loud speaker, he began to cry. While I was waiting to shake his hand, I wondered if I should stand there ready to catch him if he fainted. He didn't faint, but was totally speechless while tears streamed down his cheeks.

It was beautiful watching him while listening to the students cheering. Believe me, it was a memorable ceremony. Faculty, as well as many students, came up to wish him well. I think I, too, had a few tears during this graphic demonstration of how much Lupe was loved at this school.

When I went into my classroom the next period, I found the students were still wound up with happiness and excitement. Knowing any lesson would be a lost cause, I suggested we all make up white sheets of poster paper with "Congratulations Lupe" and the date marking it "Lupe Uribe Day" at the top. They all went around to the various classrooms getting the kids to sign their names. We divided up the papers so each student was able to carry one to get the autographs. They reported back with all the papers signed. I took them to the office and had Hank give them to Lupe.

It was a wonderful day, and I was proud of our faculty and student body. Such an activity builds "esprit de Corps" at the school. The next week at the school board meeting, they called for Lupe to suspend his duties and come to the meeting to receive their congratulations.

Lupe was and is one of my best friends. His kids have done wonders with their lives. One even gave his father a kidney.

Since one of his kids is the equipment manager of the Arizona Diamondbacks, this gift was acknowledged by the television announcers during a game.

We know it is not only teachers who are remembered fondly by students long after they have graduated. Lupe proved they remember other people who help make the "alma mater" loved. I think both Vaughn and I, being old Marines, loved the day the most. The two Marines who came up from Phoenix said the ceremony was unique and sensational, and they would use this day to explain to young people about Marine pride.

> "When you do a thing, do it with all your might. Put your whole soul into it. Stamp it with your own personality . . . Nothing great was ever achieved without enthusiasm," Ralph Waldo Emerson.

Chapter 21

Teachers often hear they shouldn't have chosen teaching as a career because of low pay. Those who regard money as the "be all and the end all" for motivation tell us we are suckers but in softer words. They do this by implication, but the criticism is there. Most teachers I've known didn't have money as their prime motivation. We often heard the old chestnut, "Those who can, do; those who can't, teach." I grew very tired of hearing it, but I tried to keep my cool. Of course, I believe teachers should be paid a fair wage for what they do. I'm glad "idealists" who enter the teaching profession say teaching children is one of the most important and rewarding tasks there is.

Christa McAuliffe, the wonderful young teacher who President Reagan selected to be the first "civilian" to voyage into space in 1986 probably said it best, "I affect the future; I teach." As most readers know, Christa's space craft blew up shortly after takeoff. I cried when it happened, and I cry whenever I think about it. I believe the spirit of Christa walks behind all teachers and smiles when her spirit sees children learning to think.

Besides the idealism teaching requires, most of us found we couldn't find a more interesting and satisfying job.

I looked forward to going to work nearly every day because I knew each day would bring new experiences, and these experiences would bring something to remember. I firmly believe, "the more I learned, the less I knew." I know when I retired I was a much better teacher than I was at the beginning of my career, and I realized I always had a lot to learn.

I once told a group of young people preparing for the teaching profession they would be on the biggest adventure of their lives and one they would enjoy and never forget. To be a good teacher takes hard work, an outgoing personality, and a huge sense of humor. A good teacher is one who will continually adapt to new techniques. There are students in classrooms who will learn in spite of peer pressure on them to ignore classroom activities. There are also those who resist learning for one reason or another. It is the teacher's job to motivate them into trying and to keep trying. To do this, the teacher must be part teacher, part actor, and part friend.

I had a student once who got a low <u>F</u> on a test. I asked him if he had studied. He assured me he had studied for over an hour before taking the test. I then told him perhaps he should change his method of studying since his old method didn't work. He responded, "No one cares how I do." I assured him I cared. No teacher can succeed with every student, but he should never stop trying. All young teachers should know it might be they who light the spark which changes a student's life for the better. Often reluctant students want to change, but they sometimes put up a front indicating they don't care. This is just an excuse they can use in case they don't succeed. Teachers should watch for the student who wants help but is afraid to ask for it. This is the type who makes teaching hard work, but when hard work succeeds, it's very satisfying.

As a teacher, I had a lot of fun and always tried to make each day in the classroom pleasurable for students. Veteran teachers can often tell by a sparkle in a pupil's eyes if the lesson is reaching him. Sometimes the sparkle comes not because of the teacher but from a classmate.

> "When the uncapped potential of a student meets the liberating art of a teacher, a miracle unfolds,"
> Mary Hatwood Futrell

Chapter 22

When I was teaching Arizona history, we often had little dramas in the classroom to reinforce some of the lessons. Watching history being made sticks with pupils a bit longer than a sentence or two in a text book. In one of these short dramas, we dramatized what might have happened if General Crook went to the White House to discuss with President Grant his appointment to end the Apache war in Arizona. We set the scene in the "ante room" while General Crook waited for an audience with the President. I gave the class this bare-bones outline. They wrote and acted their own scripts. They had a good time amplifying this scenario. When the General sat down, he was immediately joined by a large "cowboy" type. "I understand you'll be the new cavalry commander in Arizona, Sir."

"Yes, the President appointed me. We are old friends from Civil War times."

"General, I'm here to tell the President and you how to handle the Apaches in Arizona. I recently lost two sons when the Apaches attacked my ranch just outside of Tucson. I want every Apache wiped from the state of Arizona. They are nothing but murdering barbarians!"

"I'm sorry for your loss," the general replied.

"Then I hope you and the army will do something to drive Indians out of Arizona," the rancher said as he walked back across the room.

When the general was again alone, a woman crossed the room and sat down next to him. "You mustn't pay any attention to such talk, Sir. The Apaches are like children who need to be taught better ways. We should give them blankets and food. Then they wouldn't be mischievous like some misguided children."

When the general thanked her, another man came over to him. "That old lady thinks if we spoil the Indians they will grow up to be solid citizens. I don't believe that's the way, General."

"And what is the right way, Sir?"

"The right way is to get to know them and treat them fair. Give them the land they love and are defending. They are like an army which will stop its attacks if we can work out reasonable terms."

After the students said their versions of the "ante room" scenes, they changed a few lines and improvised a few more to add humor and flavor to the scene. We had a discussion about General Crook's task and how he went about it. We were able to "fatten up" the lesson in the history book by acting out these little dramas. They were fun to do and there was lots of participation. I knew they were thinking about Arizona in the 1880s and 90s. Seeing an issue from all sides is, I think, what history is all about. I believe the General treated the Apaches so well they trusted him to honor his promises to them. Of course, the government treated them horribly after they surrendered by sending them to Florida where many died. Geronimo, the last warrior to surrender, died at Fort Sill, Oklahoma, where he continued to hope he could return to his beloved Arizona mountains. I pointed out our treatment of them was quite similar to the way the Jews were treated in Germany during "the Holocaust."

During one of my classes in Arizona history, we were discussing the beginning of the Apache war. We had read about young Lieutenant Bascome when he came to the Overland Stage station near Apache Springs in the Chiricahua Mountains of southern Arizona. I explained how Hollywood and books often talked about what Bascome did and how they often presented different points of view. From the back row, a big tackle on the football team raised his hand asking, "Why can't we have a little play about what happened?"

"That's a good idea," I agreed. "Let's do it."

The same voice from the back then asked, "Who's going to direct it?"

"You are. Now your job is to get the little play written and then assign roles. You need Lieutenant Bascome and some soldiers and Cochise and some Apaches. You also need a few persons who run the stage stop. Tom Jeffords is perhaps a key player. James Stewart played him in the movie *Broken Arrow*."

"We probably won't be able to give roles to the whole class, will we?"

"Probably not," I responded, "The rest can be lurking Redskins."

He had lots of volunteers to take the various roles and to write the "screenplay." Then they got to work in earnest. Soon they had a script and began to put the drama together. One day I let them go to the auditorium to have a rehearsal. The people who were not in the play sat down in the hall above the auditorium to watch the acting on the stage.

I looked up and saw Superintendent Barbarick walk over to the hall sitters. "What are you kids doing out of class? Where are you supposed to be this period?"

A girl named Beth Martin who would be valedictorian when she graduated, said, "We're from Mr. Gabrielson's Arizona history class. We're rehearsing a little play. We are redskins *lurking* about, and we have to practice *lurking*."

From where I was sitting in the auditorium, I saw Hank stand there a moment speechless. Then he turned around and walked away.

The *lurking* Redskins came down into the auditorium laughing. "You should have seen the look on Mr. Barbarick's face when we said we were practicing *lurking*."

The Broadway critics would have panned the play, but for a classroom project, it was a smash hit. The kids all understood about the start of the Apache war which lasted about 40 years in Arizona before peace came. When I gave the chapter test, everyone passed. Sure this played heck with my lesson plans for the week, but it was worth it. I know the *lurking* Redskins will remember the look on Hank's face probably better than they'll remember the Bascome Affair.

I was saddened a couple of years later when I heard my wonderful director had been killed in an automobile accident. He was one of my very favorite students.

Many students think history is a dull subject because history text books are often dull. I think those little dramas make history come alive.

> "Good teaching is one-fourth preparation and three-fourths theater," Gail Godwin

Chapter 23

Some teachers don't believe in "extra credit." Their argument is often a sound one. They argue they present the material, and when tests are given, everyone in the class is rated on the same standard and given equal credit. Some claim giving extra credit is unfair since *everyone* didn't have a chance to take a shot at it. However, I believed in it and still do. My argument is if a student is willing to step on a little different path, he should be rewarded for his initiative and willingness to do some additional work. I often gave students a little reward if they memorized lines of poetry which they found memorable and inspirational, but I made sure *all the students in the class were given the same opportunity.*

One year on the last day of school, I was making out semester grades and totaling them up for a final grade. On about the fourth record on which I put the final grade and percentages in the book, I inked in an <u>F</u> because he had earned only 57%, and a minimum of 60% was required to pass. Then I noticed in the attendance column he had attended every day—never even being tardy. Thinking for a moment or two, I decided to give him 5% for perfect attendance. At the same time, I would give all students with a perfect record the same grade boost. It would raise some Cs to Bs as well as getting others a passing grade. I gave those who only missed two days or less three percentage points. I thought it might be a small incentive to improve attendance as well as boosting grades. I continued doing this until I retired. I sincerely believe it did improve attendance. I also believe it might show students good attendance is important in the work place. My argument was companies give bonuses for extra good performances and the military rewards heroes with medals for duty above what is expected.

As I write this, I remember vividly a time when I used extra credit and perhaps changed a student's outlook on education. One day, a few weeks before the end of the semester, a senior came to me and asked, "My counselor asked me to ask you if I had a chance to pass. If I pass this class, I'll be able to graduate." He probably knew in advance what my answer would be, but he hoped it would turn into a pleasant surprise.

I knew he was very much on the highway to failure since he had done little. He hardly ever passed a test or asked or answered a question in class discussions. Besides, his attendance was horrible. "I don't think you can pass. You've dug yourself into a hole so deep I don't think anything can happen to make passing possible. You need to take this course over in summer school and do better work there."

He looked down and asked, "What if I got <u>As</u> on all the tests until the end of the year?"

"I'm sorry, but I still don't think that will help."

"What if I came every day, got all <u>As</u> and did a whole lot of extra credit?"

"What do you have in mind for extra credit?" I asked. This was a course in Arizona history, so the field was almost limitless.

"Anything you want, Mr. Gabrielson. Please let me at least try."

I said, "We have recently studied how the Apache wars started near where Fort Bowie is located. What if you went down there on the weekend and talked to the people at the fort and took lots of pictures and then gave a *super* report to the class? It might at least help, but I can't guarantee it."

"I'll talk to my dad. He'll take me down there. He wants me to graduate very much because a bunch of relatives are coming. How far is it to Fort Bowie?"

"It's probably over 250 miles. You go to Wilcox and signs will take you to the fort. You have to walk in since they don't allow cars to leave the parking lot. It's about a mile or so to the fort, but you'll pass by the Overland Stage station where Lieutenant Bascom shot some relatives of Cochise. You might remember we studied it a month ago. It was the incident which started our last Indian War. You'll pass Apache Springs where two battles of Apache Pass were fought. If you do this, you must attend every day from now on, and get <u>A</u>s on all the tests including the final. Do you understand the rules?"

"Yes, Sir! Thanks for giving me a chance." I think he smiled for the first time since the beginning of the semester. He offered his hand and we shook to seal the deal.

His father did drive him and a friend to Fort Bowie over the weekend. When he came in Monday, he was exuberant. I asked him how he liked the fort. He replied, "It was wonderful! We wandered all over down there, and they gave me lots of stuff to read. It was very interesting." Again, I saw him smile.

"When will you give your report to the class?"

He replied, "When the pictures I took are developed. We had them turned into slides so the class can see some of the things I saw." Every day I saw him smile and he worked hard on every lesson. A couple of his other teachers reported a dramatic change in his attitude.

I'm proud to say he gave a beautiful report with an enthusiasm he couldn't have faked. The slides were given to me for next year's classes to enjoy. He got <u>A</u>s on all the remaining tests and a <u>B</u> on the final. I didn't see his parents at the graduation ceremony, but I'm sure they were there. It was wonderful to see him cross the stage and receive his diploma. I also believe he learned more in those final days of his senior year than he learned the whole year. I don't know if that little spark changed him a lot, but I hope so. In addition, the class developed a greater interest in the Apache wars in Arizona.

Do I believe in giving students a bit of help if they need it and are willing to do it? I sure do! Those little sparks often light the big lamp of learning. I remember fondly some of my favorite teachers who gave me a little extra push when I needed it.

> "The important thing is not so much that every child should be taught, as that every child should be given the wish to learn," John Lubbock

Chapter 24

Since I retired, I heard many times, "You're lucky you retired when you did. The kids today are unmanageable, and the school doesn't teach kids much anymore. Also the school can't discipline students as they did in the past because of new laws. *They don't teach no grammar no more.*"

I smile at some of modern education's critics. True, school curricula have changed, but changes don't necessarily mean change is bad. I always had a paragraph on my desk to remind me about education and the change in kids.

> *The children now love luxury; they show disrespect for elders and love to chatter in place of exercise.*
> *Children are tyrants, not servants of their households. They no longer rise when their elders enter a room.*
> *They contradict their parents, chatter before company, gobble up sweets at the table, cross their legs and tyrannize over their teachers.*

That little speech is often attributed to Socrates, a philosopher in ancient Greece. I'm not sure today's children are much different than those discussed by Socrates in the Fifth Century, B.C. I always enjoyed my students' reactions when I read Socrates' words aloud to them. They smiled at "finding out" they aren't much different than kids were in their parents' day.

Before 1949, only about 50% of graduates from the eighth grade went on to high school. Then there were lots of jobs for young people without a high school or college diploma, and, as a result, high schools only had to cope with the brightest and motivated students. After World War II, colleges and universities became crowded because of the G.I. Bill which did a lot to change education in America. I know I, at least, would never have attended college without the help of the G.I. Bill. The changes in American education were staggering because many of the new graduates had little sympathy for some outmoded traditional beliefs, and they spoke up about those beliefs. No one wants to continue teaching students how to fight sabre-toothed tigers now that none exist.

When I began teaching, I noticed many of the younger teachers were approaching the subject matter differently. I started with the conservative approach. I had students diagram sentences to enable them to "name the parts." Some eagerly approached this exercise while drawing beautiful diagrams. However, many students had a lot of trouble with this. I tried my best to make it fun by having them diagram familiar sentences such as our "Pledge to the Flag." From this, they certainly learned what a prepositional phrase looks like, but did that knowledge enable them to use those phrases effectively when writing? Maybe I was teaching things because they were taught to me in my school days solely because of tradition.

Gradually, I stopped doing those things in favor of "sentence combining." I don't think, however, teachers can get away without instructing students in <u>some</u> traditional lessons. I laugh when I think of my oral exams at NAU as I completed my Education Specialist Degree. The Dean of Students was on the panel quizzing me. He asked, "What does research say about the knowledge of grammar and the ability to write effectively?"

My answer was research found little coordination between writing and the knowledge of grammar.

"Then why do high schools continue to teach traditional grammar?"

"Facetiously, Doctor, we do it because colleges and universities test students on their knowledge of traditional grammar." I realized by the look on his face I had given the wrong answer. I came back hurriedly with, "But research definitely shows good writing doesn't <u>necessarily</u> depend on knowledge of grammar." I hoped he wouldn't blackball me because of my facetious response. He didn't and I passed the test. The head of the English Department smiled and gave me a "thumbs up."

After I retired from high school teaching, I continued on a limited basis by teaching English 101 and 102 at our local community college. There were always some students in my classes who <u>wanted</u> a lesson or two in traditional grammar simply because they felt they would need it, and hadn't received even a small bit of it in middle or high school. I did spend a class or two by pointing out "grammar" is largely vocabulary or "naming the parts." We went over the 25 or so most common names. I hope those few lessons gave them the confidence to write more effectively and meet any demands they might face as they advanced in education.

As an exercise, I had them write a five-sentence essay using a different grammatical beginning for each sentence. This exercise showed them varying the beginning of sentences made their writing more interesting.

I think it is worth knowing some traditional methods are good and still work. I think this is true not only in English classes but in all subjects. However, students should know some of the "rules or doctrines of correctness" are no longer valid because our language is constantly changing and growing. I don't think auto shop classes need to spend a lot of time on lessons explaining how to fix carburetors since fuel injection has replaced carburetors. (They should be aware of the fact older cars need help with carburetors.) Changed methods need to be made in all disciplines—not just English.

We should also be aware text books are very often out of date—almost as soon as they are printed. When I was teaching *King Arthur Legends*, I always noted most texts still credit the "wrong" Malory as the author of *Morte D'Arthur*. Hopefully teachers now don't insist Columbus discovered America. It took a while for humans to learn the earth wasn't flat as the older texts claimed. Henry Ford once said," All history is bunk." In many cases, he was right.

> "Parents must acknowledge that the schooling, which will be best for their children in the 21st century, must be very different from the schooling they experienced themselves," Andy Hargreaves and Michael Fullan

Chapter 25

Over the years I have attended many public meetings where controversial subjects were brought up. I've watched people in the audiences who wanted to speak up but sat on their hands in silence. Many of these maintained they would have or should have spoken up but were afraid they would make a mistake in language usage and look foolish. In my classes, one of the prime lessons I worked on teaching was language so people will speak up without fear. I believe "speaking up" is the essence of democracy.

Students need to know there are various levels of speaking, and one should speak the level of English which makes the listener or listeners comfortable. First, there is the *intimate* level spoken only by family members or lovers' pet language to each other. Then there is the *informal* level which is spoken generally. As one of my college teachers said, "Saying 'It is I,' is correct, but its use may get you blackballed in your social clubs. Being overly "correct" often makes the speaker sound like a stuffed shirt.

Then there is the *technical* level used in workplaces such as the military, software development companies, etc. *Texting* is developing a whole different way to speak and write. Finally there is the *formal* level which is used in most writing and, perhaps, at a White House dinner. It is always wise to speak in the comfort zone of listeners even if your old English teacher might not approve. When writers use dialogue in papers and books, the words used should match what the character would use. This even applies to profanity.

Instead of traditional grammar lessons, I thought teaching *usage* was more important. Again, one of my college teachers once said, "You teach them the difference between the words *to*, *too*, and *two*, and we'll take care of the rest." English teachers can't do this alone. I believe <u>all</u> teachers should use language as well as they are able. Again, students learn more by example than they do by text books or lectures. When a teacher or father uses swear words frequently, it should be no surprise youngsters imitate what they hear.

Keith West, my boss in Jerome, continually used the word *irregardless* when he spoke whether it was in front of the whole student body or in conversation. Once when I was in his office, I said, "Keith, you use the word *irregardless* a lot when you really mean *regardless*. Your word doesn't make sense to an English teacher. It's what we call a *double negative*."

He thought a minute and said, "I've always used it, but I see what you mean." Afterwards he smiled down on me when he got it right when speaking.

When I taught college composition, I wrote about 20 things on the board which were important in writing because in those things mistakes were so apparent. "Seldom will anyone find fault if you spell Albuquerque wrong, but don't get *their*, *there*, or *they're* wrong."

The current AIMS test in writing has become a big hurdle for some. It's used as an exit test from high school in Arizona, and one must pass it to graduate. The things the judges look for are the most obvious mistakes in usage—not grammar. Misplacing a comma is not as serious as when students write *hear* when *here* is the word needed.

English teachers should, I believe, have drills in usage and vocabulary. It pays off when students are faced with an important test of their writing or knowledge of their language.

One story I told on myself brought this home. Every Friday, my English 101 teacher in college read aloud the best composition which had been submitted and talked about the things that made it good. During the semester, she read a number of them but never one of mine. However, one assignment she made was to write an essay using imagery. I worked hard through the week writing one using an old tramp steamer going by the coast. I tried to make every image come alive so perhaps the teacher might read it aloud on Monday. I was pleased when she did read it aloud and commented it was good in its use of imagery, but then she dropped it into the waste basket saying, "I can't give this any credit because of five misspelled words—all *thier* instead of *their*." As I tried to slither out of the room when the period ended, she caught me and asked me to report to her office the next day at 11:00. I took this as an order—not a request. I reported shaking in my shoes fearing she might drop me completely out of the English education program and suggest I change my major. She had a student desk out in the hall with several sheets of paper stapled together.

"Mr. Gabrielson, sit there and write *their* as many times as it takes to fill all these pages." Many English majors and teachers passed by while I was doing this, and everyone snickered at this "grade school" punishment. I did learn <u>I</u> before <u>E</u> wasn't always a rule to follow. I had it right when I wrote the essay, but changed it just before handing it in. I think it is often good when teachers tell about some of the stupid things they did when they were in school. It often makes lessons more memorable than text books alone.

When I was interviewing prospective teachers, I tended toward those who didn't have a "perfect" transcript with all <u>As</u>. I think those who had to struggle some might understand students struggling better.

"It's not always what you say but the way you say it."

Chapter 26

I was very proud I taught in a public high school. Today, there are many kinds of private schools, charter schools, and home-schooling. These forms of education have certain advantages over the public schools, but they may rob students of certain advantages found in a public school. Quite a few "memories" are left out of the other kind of school—memories such as school dances, pep assemblies, the concern about the "big" game, yearbooks, proms, etc.

A mother once told me, "I home school my daughter because there are *boys* in the public schools, and I don't want my daughter to get mixed up with them before she's an adult." I didn't say much to her, but I think the daughter was missing out on learning about the opposite gender early and learning how to cope with it. Part of the job of a school is to teach kids to function in a society where their mothers aren't always around to protect them.

Once, I visited a private school. The young English teacher there bragged about how advanced his students were compared to those in public schools. They were all reading "college-age" books and stories. Again, I kept my mouth shut but privately wondered when his students would read some valuable books other high school students were reading. I think education is a series of steps on a path, and kids need to experience most of the steps. Introducing students to Shakespeare, Homer, Chaucer and others is good because classic authors provide valuable steps on the path of learning. The key word is, of course, *introducing*.

Various types of schools answer real needs. Some kids can't function well in the public school environment but are getting their education in other types of schools. I know I'm very prejudiced toward a school with a teacher up front conducting a lively discussion of questions brought up in the work. I loved having kids in my classroom all keyed up about the big game or dance as well as the lesson. Once I even was responsible for the cheerleaders changing a cheer they had learned at "state" during the summer. The basketball season was in full swing, and one of the cheers yelled before a jump ball was, "JUMP HIGH, JUMP LOW, COME ON JERRY, LET'S GO." One of our pretty cheerleaders came into class one day and I jokingly asked, "Your cheer rhymes, but do you really want the players to JUMP LOW?"

She responded they learned the cheer at state and *all* the schools were using it. She apparently thought her response should be the end of the discussion. I smiled and walked away before she really got defensive about their cheers. About a week later she came to class smiling and said, "We changed the cheer because our sponsor said you were right because jumping low doesn't make sense." That memory has stuck with me for a long time, and I hope it became a pleasant memory for the pretty cheerleader as well. I hope she learned "state" isn't always right.

Again, a big part of education is to have fun while learning valuable lessons which sometimes are not taught by textbooks or computers.

Today, many colleges and universities have crowded classrooms on the lower levels with classes of about 600 students or more and graduate assistants to grade and mark papers. In these classrooms, there is no time for questions or discussion. Now some of these lessons are taught by TV instead of a teacher in the room. My compliments to technology, but I think students are being short changed. I hope high schools don't follow along with all the trends of technology but leave time and room for discussion and laughter.

We need to leave students with pleasant memories as well as having them master lessons only from textbooks. I had fun when I was a high school student and have fond memories of Bisbee High and its wonderful teaching staff. Many of them certainly "affected the future." Since many of us wanted to be teachers who try to affect the future, I think we owe today's young people the same opportunities for pleasant memories such as we had.

> "An education that does not strive to promote the fullest and most thorough understanding of the world is not worthy of the name," George S. Counts

Chapter 27

While teachers love to recall favorite students and favorite lessons, there is always the other side of the coin. It is also extremely difficult to forget failures. I can recall many students who wouldn't allow me to get into their lives. I'm sure quite a few teachers quit the profession because these failures became too much for them to bear. Some blame the students for failure while at least part of the blame might be on their own shoulders.

I have written about some of my happiest days and favorite lessons in school, and those are the ones which made my choice of teaching for many years so wonderful. I know of many people who are happy they have lots of money and power because of their choice of jobs, but I don't think most of them become happier in their lives than does a teacher who hears from a student: "You made a great difference in my life." Money doesn't mean nearly as much as hearing that. All the long-term teachers who are my friends would certainly agree with me.

The smiles, the laughter, the look in their eyes when something a teacher says or does has struck a cord is without equal. I remember once when a student came up to me after class and said, "Mr. Gabrielson, you mixed me all up today."

I replied, "Great! That's my job. Thank you for telling me."

Then she chuckled and said, "I guess that's right. See you tomorrow and you'll probably do it again to me."

One of the best things a teacher can do is "mix up" students. I believe mixing them up is another definition of learning. Of course, sometimes students resent it when a cherished belief is challenged, but it might cause some thinking. An example of this concerned my wife.

An English instructor from NAU offered an evening class in Cottonwood titled, "The Development of the Novel." My wife, Carroll, said she'd like to take it, so I stayed home with the kids. Everything went well for a few weeks as the course progressed. She liked the teacher and the books they were reading and discussing.

But one night she came home steaming. She said the professor "ruined" the book they had read because he talked about things in the book she or many others didn't see or think about when they read it.

"I'm not going next week because we're discussing <u>Catch 22</u>. I love that book because it's so funny." She threw her book and notebook down on a chair and just fumed probably expecting me to sympathize with her.

I listened to her rant and rave for awhile hiding a smile. Then I made a mistake. I said, "He made waves in your little world, did he?" Then I had to retreat to the bathroom because she got angry. She simply transferred her anger to me—away from the professor.

She came back to the bedroom still shouting, and I finally came out and said, "The professor is going to call <u>Catch 22</u> a brilliant anti-war novel, perhaps the best ever, but let's work on an interpretation which might be more than he expects.

All week we worked on her *special* interpretation which might "make waves in *his* little world."

When she came home after the class, her eyes were sparkling. Her grin was as wide as the Grand Canyon. "You got your ideas into the class discussion then?"

"No. He talked the whole period about the book, and I didn't get a chance."

"Then why are you smiling?"

"I went up after class and told him about our thoughts. He said, "You are right on the money, but it's a bit too complex for this group. You certainly earn an <u>A</u> for it though."

The professor's job was to mix his students up a little and he did a great job. I wish I could tell him so.

I'm sitting here at my computer alone, but I have lots of company—many of the students I had in various schools and classrooms are still 14 to 18 in my mind.

I smile when I recall a moment in history class when I said, "There will be only two dates to remember in this course. One will be July 4, 1776, and the other is February 14, 1912. I will not throw a lot of dates at you to mix you up."

One student said "I think we all know about July 4th, but what's the other one?"

"It's Arizona's birthday, but it will only appear when we study Arizona history in the second semester. But those dates will be on a test, and if anyone misses them, they will have to march us down to the auditorium and lead us in the fight song in front of the principal's office." My threat was met with laughter because they "knew" no one would miss such an easy question.

I warned them again the day before the test on the American Revolution, "Be careful, one of the two dates will be on the test." The room echoed with laughter again.

The next day, as I collected the finished tests, I discovered two students managed to miss July 4, 1776. I named them and one of them was my daughter. "I DID NOT MISS IT!" She retorted angrily from the back of the room. My daughter flounced up to my desk repeating, "I DID NOT!" When I showed her she had written 1976, she turned beet red. Both of them marched us to the auditorium and led the class in the fight song in front of the whole front office staff since they all poured out to see what was going on. I know my daughter never forgot the day or date again, and I doubt any of my students did either. When I taught Arizona history the second semester, no one missed our birthday.

I know kids have fond memories of things they learned in school if instruction is mixed with a little fun and laughter. Teachers also need a laugh now and then. Students often laugh when a teacher is willing to do things showing his class he was no different from the students today.

Once when I was discussing one of Shakespeare's plays, a student came in tardy and slipped into a seat in the back row. He was wearing a baseball cap which he didn't take off. When he sat down, many students began to chuckle.

Not knowing what the chuckling was about, I walked to the back still discussing some point in <u>Macbeth</u>. As I approached the young man, the chuckling became a bit louder. "We take off our hats in the classroom," I whispered to the tardy student.

When he removed his cap, we all saw a brand new "Mohawk" haircut. I smiled and rubbed my hand over the Mohawk part in the middle of his head. "You have a Mohawk haircut. I remember I had one when I was in high school."

A gasp of surprise, shock and disbelief escaped from most of the students. Then it turned to happy laughter when a girl asked, "YOU had a Mohawk, Mr. Gabrielson?"

After the laughter died down, we went back to <u>Macbeth</u> sort of refreshed. It was a lot of fun to even suggest I acted up in school.

By the way, my Mohawk only lasted one day. Coach Dicus told several of us on the football team the "Mohawks" would have to go by the next day's football practice. We all went to a barber shop and the young Mohawks got scalped.

> "The whole art of teaching is only the art of awakening the natural curiosity of the mind for the purpose of satisfying it afterwards," Anatole France.

Chapter 28

Julie Andrews sings of her favorite things in the hit Broadway musical, *The Sound of Music.* I suppose every teacher has a few favorite lessons. I know I did. In fact, I had quite a few of them. When it comes to favorite lessons, teachers love it when they become favorites of their students as well.

When I coached football, some of my favorite things were not really on the football field. I had mostly 9th graders on the squad, and in those days, JV football was played on Saturday afternoons. I had a good time taking those boys on road trips. On our way to Winslow one Saturday, we stopped in the forest just outside Flagstaff to eat a snack. The team had a few minutes to wander around in the trees before we re-boarded the bus. One of the boys stopped to thank me for stopping. "Coach, I've never been in the forest before. It's sure great."

"Don't you stop when your family goes to Flagstaff?"

"No, my dad just drives through here, and we have never stopped. Those big trees are really something. I'm going to ask Dad to stop next time we go through this forest. I bet my little sister will like it too."

We usually had an after-game meal in a restaurant. Many players told me they had never eaten in a restaurant before. New experiences like walking around in a forest or eating in a restaurant sometimes are better and more important than playing the game.

In World History, my favorite lessons were set in ancient Greece. I loved studying the Trojan War. This was an area introducing mythology and the first experience with Homer's great stories. These tales were often the first time kids met Achilles, Hector, Helen, Penelope, Mentor, and many others. Those stories offer romance, adventure and mystery. I also knew I was preparing them for further study as they progressed in education and reading. I'd hate for them to go to college not knowing about the huge, wooden Trojan horse.

In American History, I spent a lot of time on the Revolutionary War because it offers so much to study and think about. The battles of Lexington and Concord are so interesting because that day in April was when the "shot heard 'round the world" was fired. An interesting question arises: Which side fired it? I tried to make those immortal figures such as Revere, Adams, Franklin, Washington, Jefferson, Arnold, Lafayette, and many others come alive for the class as they had for me when I was in high school.

It was a treat to discuss the "whole" career of Benedict Arnold and his beautiful wife Peggy. I think Shakespeare's words apply to the "hero of Saratoga" as well as to Julius Caesar. "The good that men do is oft interred with their bones. The evil lives after them."

When I taught American Literature, I loved reading and talking about the stories of Hawthorne, Poe, and Mark Twain. I very much wanted the young readers to develop favorites of their own. I also liked to dramatize things like Patrick Henry's fiery speech and Lincoln's *Gettysburg Address*.

English Literature was like a large garden offering many trails to follow. When we chose a new textbook, it contained several essays on the English language by Dr. L.D. Benson of Harvard. His contribution was writing a two- or three-page history as the language developed through the various ages. I liked them because they told in simple language how our language develops and changes. Those short essays were also good for précis writing. But I also liked them because Larry Benson had been a Marine Corps buddy of mine in Korea.

During the Medieval period, I always paused at the prologue to the *Canterbury Tales* written by Geoffrey Chaucer. It was fun to explore his characterizations of the people in the society of that time. I think he inspired students to use their imagination so well they walked with the Pilgrims from

London to Canterbury listening to the wonderful stories. My favorite tale was *The Wife of Bath's Story* because of its wonderful ending.

One cold, rainy day in Cottonwood, I was teaching some dull lesson in English. I chanced to look out the window, and I saw the fog rising from the Verde River. It was a beautiful sight—so beautiful I immediately asked the class to put away their books. They looked startled but then I explained, "Today is a perfect day to start the Arthurian legends. Look out the window at the fog rising from the river and imagine you're in Fifth Century England at a place called <u>Camelot</u>. We're going there starting now."

"But we didn't bring our literature books," a student pointed out while still looking puzzled.

"Never mind," I said, "we'll wing it for today." I looked forward to teaching this wonderful legend. We talked about the differences among fairy tales, folktales, myths and legends. I mentioned legends begin with a <u>germ</u> of truth, but sometimes become mythic. I wrote the names of principal characters o the board, and the students copied them and put a few descriptive sentences by each.

The next day they ditched their language books and brought their literature books. I came to school early the next morning and cranked out some copies of parts of T.H. White's book, *The Sword and the Stone.* I also brought other reference books from my home. In the literature book we had White's chapter when Arthur pulled the sword from the stone. We also had some portions of Tennyson, Malory and others who wrote about the legend. Teaching those great stories was fun for me and, I hope, fun and instructive for the students. I allowed three weeks for the legend. There were weekly tests and some writing assignments. Quite often former students came back saying the legend was their favorite lesson from junior English. I hope English teachers still use these legends while studying literature.

One year as we began school, a pretty Japanese girl came to class. She was a very frightened exchange student. As I was signing her in, I asked where in Japan she was from. She replied, "Osaka." I told her I had been there and found it was a very beautiful city. Almost immediately, she lost her frightened look and smiled. Through the year, she worked diligently learning English and studying things like the Arthurian legends. Once she told the class this legend was big in the schools of Japan. I think the entire class was amazed that the whole world knew of it; and, I think, this induced them to study it harder. Toward the end of the year, she handed me a beautiful, leather-bound book of the legend printed in Japanese saying, "Mr. Gabrielson, my parents wanted me to give you this."

She explained, "You probably can't read it because in Japan, we start at the back of the book and read pages from the bottom." I've never read a word from the book, but it's one of my treasures. Every time I look at it, I am reminded of the wonderful Japanese girl and the joy we had discussing the Round Table.

> "I believe that children learn best when given the opportunity to taste, feel, see, hear, manipulate, discover, sing, and dance their way through learning,"
> Katy Goldman

Chapter 29

Sometimes teachers don't want to teach subjects "out of their expertise," but I looked forward to it. I think teaching something different helps refresh teachers. I loved to teach Shakespeare and Chaucer along with other great writers, but I never wanted my teaching to become so routine it became stale. When the State Department of Education passed a law mandating schools must teach a semester of World History and a semester of World Geography, I was delighted. I immediately asked for the World History classes.

Mr. Barber, the principal, said, "No, I have watched you teach Shakespeare and you should stay with it. I have history majors who can and will teach a semester of World History, and Mr. Green has volunteered to teach World Geography. Green, being a science major is qualified. You're an English major—not a history major."

I almost begged him for the chance to teach something a bit different from the stuff I had been teaching. "Mr. Barber, I have traveled extensively and have read widely on world history—maybe studied it more than some history majors. In addition, I had such a strong history minor in college it almost became an additional major."

After a few days, he called both Tom and I into his office and said, "The new freshman class will need five sections of each of these subjects. Will you teach all the sections?" He looked at both of us while he waited for our answer. Since we had talked about it, he didn't have to wait long.

We both agreed and then he asked, "Will you give up your current classrooms and teach in a portable classroom because one of the teachers doesn't want to be in a portable?"

We both happily agreed because our classrooms would be back to back, and the switching at the end of the semester would be easy for us and for the students.

I knew I had to bone up on some parts of history which I hadn't studied before. While I was learning a great deal to fill the gaps, I knew I was off on a great new adventure. I believed I could handle the stories of ancient Greece well but was weak on the "fertile crescent" in Persia (now Iraq), Egypt, Israel and many developments which shaped our world today. The studying was fun. I found many of my freshmen had difficulty reading, so it was a challenge to teach younger kids who had wide differences in ability. One day we came to a chapter in the book that was broken down into discussions of several cultural groups in the Middle East before the Christian era. Each group had only a few paragraphs written about it. I assigned each student to choose only one of the groups and write a précis of the main ideas. None of the sections was longer than a few paragraphs, so the assignment wasn't going to be too daunting for anyone. I had previously given them the same exercises in putting the main ideas in their own words. As they read aloud from the text in class, I sometimes found they were strong in pronouncing words phonetically but weak when it came to understanding what the main ideas were.

As I was taking roll the next morning, Mr. Barber came for a "surprise evaluation." He sat in back with a notebook open to take notes. I collected the papers and drew a line under the last sentence the student had written, so he couldn't add to it after the précis reading. I then passed the papers back with my initials on them. This was to prevent any student from writing one in class if he hadn't turned one in. Then I called up each student and had him or her read their précis aloud. Each one generated questions and discussion. The class went very well. I again collected the papers for grading. This exercise also gave the students a little practice on speaking before a group. Most freshmen have little experience in public speaking.

After the period ended, Mr. Barber asked, "What was it you had them do?"

I told him a précis is a short summary of the main ideas written in their own words and having them do this increased their comprehension of the material.

"Would you conduct an in-service work shop about this method of teaching during the next teacher's meeting?"

I was a little surprised he had never used this method when he taught. I did conduct the seminar as I gave some short material to the staff to write a précis. We had fun with it, but I was surprised some non-English teachers were a bit weak in putting poetry into their own words. Of course, it had been a long time since they had studied poetry if they weren't English majors.

For the classroom, I obtained menus of many different countries' special foods and hung them around the room for students to read. Every time we went to a new type of restaurant, I asked for a menu. It was fun watching the students read and discuss them. (Sometimes World History concerns food.) We had menus from such diverse places as Greece, Morocco, India and Peru. Local restaurants supplied Chinese, Mexican and German menus.

Many times Tom Green and I went to Phoenix together on Friday nights to see a baseball game and eat at an ethnic restaurant. One evening we went to a real fancy Greek restaurant with a gorgeous menu. I asked the waitress if I could have the insert to take to my class. She replied, "No, these menus are very expensive and we can't let patrons take them." She then took the menus away.

As we were leaving, the woman sitting near us handed me a complete menu which she had taken and hidden after she overheard my request. "Here, put this under your shirt and take it to your class."

"I don't want to, "I replied. "I'm afraid she'd catch me since she knows I wanted one."

"Wait for us outside. I'm going to stick this under my belt and I'll give it to you in the parking lot."

That menu became the star of the classroom and drew many visitors.

Some of my students went to Phoenix to experience ethnic restaurants, and many attended the annual Greek Festival. All in all I had fun teaching World History because most of my students were, like me, experiencing a new adventure.

Again extra credit produced big dividends. One student made a beautiful model of the path the Nile takes through Egypt. She put in mountains, pyramids, and crops along the river. It was about 4 feet wide and 8 feet long on plywood. She had worked hard painting this project in art class and at home. It was very apparent she had done a lot of studying of the Nile. Of course, when the test came, she got an <u>A</u> on everything Egyptian. She also left the project in my room and I used it many times. In spite of teaching the Nile runs south to north, students often wrote it "runs up hill" on tests. I had to suggest no river in the whole world runs up hill in spite of what it looks like on maps.

> "The only thing new in the world is the history you do not know," Harry S. Truman.

Chapter 30

One of the best things that happened to me during my career was being selected as the Arizona representative for a Literary Criticism workshop held during the summer at the University of the Pacific in Stockton, California. It was sponsored by the NDEA. There were 50 English teachers there—one from each state. Our instructors were experts in the field, and they worked us very hard during the workshop. The most valuable thing about it for me was meeting with outstanding English teachers from all over the United States.

We had many "bull" sessions about teaching and discussed which lessons we felt worked in nearly every subject in the curricula. We were given time off during the weekends to go through the wine country where we bonded over tasting various kinds of wine. Happily for us the stewards in those tasting rooms were local English teachers doing their summer jobs. During the classes and the "bull" sessions, I learned a lot about literature and how to teach it more effectively.

When I returned to school in the fall, Mr. West suggested I hold special reading classes to be held for most, if not all, the sections of English. While I had their classes, their regular teacher helped me with the reading instruction. With Jim McLarney's help, we had a reading test at the beginning of the program and one at the end of each class attempting to measure growth. Mac was a wiz at figuring standard deviation and such to measure growth. We found the students advanced quite a bit as a result of the *intensive* program. I even wrote a thesis about it which I used for the Ed Specialist degree. It would not have been written without the skill and experience of Georgia Franklin, our beloved school secretary.

That year I didn't teach any English or history—just reading. In those classes, I was able to put into practice many of the things I had learned in discussions with those teachers I met in Stockton. The main thing—we all agreed—was to <u>teach</u> there is <u>joy</u> in reading and that joy would last a lifetime. While the intensive program was one I taught, I also taught "developmental" reading to students who were deemed below-grade level.

During the program, I saw an ad from a national reading program called "Reading is Fundamental" which would provide a bookcase stacked with 100 books of interest to students on the levels of middle school and ninth and tenth grade in high school. I talked Mr. West into letting me have it as a classroom library to encourage reading.

I didn't check out the books but let students come and take their choice with the admonition to return the book soon. The librarian came down and told me I would lose all the books without a proper checking-out procedure. I continued on the honor system even allowing students who weren't in my classes to come to get books. We started with 100 books and when I took inventory at the end of the year, we had 395 in and around the original book case. I learned making books available to kids helps them to start finding the <u>joy</u> in reading which is the principal reason I give books to kids today.

As graduation time comes around each year, many parents get angry at the school because their child won't be able to graduate. One of the reasons is because of their failure to pass the AIMS writing test. Many parents argue their child is an above-average student in everything but writing—and that is no reason to withhold a diploma. I disagree with the criticism of the school because all students are given many opportunities to take and pass the writing test. Schools offer special classes on how to pass writing the simple five-paragraph essay, but since these extra classes are optional and held after-school, many students don't take this opportunity. Parents need to place the blame where it belongs—and not blame the school.

I believe very strongly student writing should be given across the total curriculum from auto shop to zebra hunting.

A few years before I retired, Bob Cox and I traveled to the University of Arizona for a workshop on how to get <u>all</u> the teachers in the school to work with youngsters to develop their ideas in an intelligent manner. Too often the responsibility is shoveled off just to the English teachers.

The workshop was led by an English professor from Harvard who made the sessions interesting and informative. We came back to our school full of enthusiasm about this idea of the entire staff working on writing. The principal gave us an opportunity to "spread the gospel," so to speak. Later the Director of Composition at the university came up to help us.

I also attended a workshop on how to grade student writing. At this 2-day workshop, we listened to many teachers speak about how they handled marking and grading essays the students write. One interesting feature of this was each of us were given copies of about 10 student essays (no names on the papers), and we were asked to give each a letter grade and make a comment or two at the end of the essay explaining why we gave the grade we did. We found there was a wide spread among the teachers' grades. Some marked an essay <u>A</u> while others marked the same essay <u>F</u> but most fell in between those extremes.

Participants placed different values on such things as spelling, punctuation, and usage. Others marked the paper with only an eye to the development of an idea clearly and effectively even though there was a mistake or two in commas, etc. From this exercise we discussed ways to improve the student writing in both ways, and to, perhaps, come to some agreement about grading fairly.

This workshop was valuable since I learned quite a bit of what other teachers were doing. I also met some of the people who might have helped score the essays for the exit tests. They told me they judged essays on appearance, word choice, mechanics and development of ideas effectively.

Certainly one thing all teachers have in common as they mark an essay is word choice. We need to warn students to write their ideas down hurriedly and then go over the paper changing words in sentences to more meaningful ones. The example almost everyone at the workshop mentioned was the nothing word <u>said.</u> There are almost an infinite number of words which can be used instead that give information about a speaker as well as identifying his words. Stephen King, one of America's most popular authors, once said good writing doesn't need a lot of adverbs if the verbs used are effective and colorful.

Again, I believe teaching students to develop and state their ideas effectively should be a mission of every teacher in the school. It is also our mission to work with all students so they can learn both writing and speaking clearly and effectively.

I used many examples of great writing to show the importance of and power of words. Ben Franklin said he learned to write by reading newspapers. He worked on the docks and obtained the papers early in the morning to read the articles written by Addison and Steele. He added he then tried to improve the original. By doing this exercise, he learned to develop ideas without the benefit of much formal education.

I encourage teachers to meet and share ideas with other teachers every chance they get. A teacher's education is never completed because they discover the more they learn, the less they know.

> "Education is a lifelong process of which schooling is only a small but necessary part. As long as one remains alive and healthy, learning can go on—and should,"
> Mortimer J. Adler

Chapter 31

Advances in technology force change of tactics in almost everything. Modern technology has certainly changed tactics in such things as warfare, politics and medicine. Armored knights gave way to gun powder and treatment of illness by witchcraft gave way to penicillin. During the 20th and 21st centuries we have developed more technological changes than any other period in human history. Things are changing so fast it's extremely difficult for most of us to keep up.

These changes have certainly affected tactics in education. I remember as a youngster teachers read the test questions to us because there was no easy and inexpensive method to make copies. Then came the mimeograph machine which could make copies of a test for everyone in the class. However, this method was soon replaced by the ditto machine which made copying easier. In its turn, ditto machines were replaced by computer-generated tests and copy machines. Today some teachers have laptop tests.

Certainly most of us can recall the time when we heard recorded music on 78 rpm vinyl discs. Then came 45 rpm, followed by 8-track machines which gave way quickly to cassettes which were replaced by CD and Mp3 players. It's possible to take our music and books with us wherever we go. We can also store a thousand songs (more than we can even listen to in a lifetime) on these devices. It would be strange, indeed, if education didn't change with new technology as well. Today's youngsters are working with computers while they're still in kindergarten or first grade. When all these new things are available to students, their lives change and teachers must accept the fact they also must change tactics. Who knows what tomorrow will bring?

Today, because of budget cuts, many subjects, which I knew and took for granted, are no longer part of the curriculum. In many ways these changes are good, but in some ways I feel we have lost something. Socrates, a teacher in ancient Greece, educated the youth of Athens by sitting on a rock near his pupils as he questioned them face to face. His method of forcing them to think was so effective those against learning forced his death by accusing him of "corrupting the youth of Athens."

The alphabet and manuscripts made it possible for more people to receive an education through reading. When printing was developed in the 15th century, schools increased the numbers of pupils because they all could have books. Of course this was opposed by those who wished the common people to remain ignorant. William Tindale, a printer in medieval England, thought it might be a good idea to print the Bible in the English language, so common people would not have to rely solely on priests to tell them what the Bible said. He was executed because he wanted the common man to be able to learn.

If such as Shakespeare or Abraham Lincoln couldn't read, the world wouldn't be quite the same. With very little formal schooling, these men managed to get an education through books and they "affected the future."

While people in my generation carried big books home from school, today's kids can carry many books at a time in their shirt pocket. Those shirt-pocket books have a bad side, however, because girls no longer need boys to carry their books home for them. I hope this doesn't interfere too much with romance.

There is no question education must change. After the first decade of the 21st century, I realized I was a teacher in a time that might be thought of as "the dark ages." In spite of not having the most modern technological tools, we think we did a good job. After all, we educated today's teachers, as they will educate tomorrow's teachers.

"The old order changeth yielding place to new,"
Alfred Lord Tennyson (Idylls of the King)

Chapter 32

When I became eligible for retirement, I had some ambivalent feelings. I discussed them with Carroll, and her response was the same as always, "It's your decision."

The first thing I wondered about was how I would feel not going to work. I always worked—even when I was very young. I knew people who retired and seemed to enjoy not working, but I also talked with others who wished they were still working—not much help there either. We had sold the Video store so a few dollars less a month on my retirement check was not a real concern.

We talked about having no anchors to keep us from traveling around the United States. We both had never seen much of it since we were both native Arizonans and hadn't traveled much because of work. Carroll said, "October is a good month to have a vacation because the weather is good almost everywhere and all the kids are back in school. There are lots of battlefields back East you can explore while I do some shopping."

I also talked with my friends on the staff as well as the Superintendent. Most of the teachers were in favor of us traveling while we were comparatively young. Mr. Barber said I could teach a couple of hours a day if I wished and have the rest of the day off. I believe coming to work only for an hour or two would be like sticking your big toe in a swimming pool without getting anything else wet. Everything about this made it a very tough decision. I felt a little like Hamlet while trying to decide. Finally I asked Mr. Barber if I could teach both sessions of World History in summer school. It would mean a couple of dollars more on my state retirement check. He agreed, and I formally retired. I think the biggest factor in my decision was wanting the experience of *not* being on a rigid schedule. Retirement might mean I could put off doing something until I felt like doing it. I imagined having no schedule ever again would be wonderful.

I was proud the graduating class dedicated the graduation ceremony to me. It was wonderful and is still one of my best memories. The teachers got together and gave me a surprise party. They passed the hat and Lupe Uribe presented me with a beautiful Marine Corps watch.

During the summer I had lots of fun teaching summer school to our incoming freshman class and telling them how much they were going to enjoy being part of Mingus. After those two sessions I wondered about what I would do.

A few days after summer school started, Tom Henry came into the classroom excitedly and whispered, "Ernie, the state retirement office just announced a window. Now we can retire with only 82 points. I just called Joan Evans in Oklahoma and told her. She said she will retire now with me." Retirement was based on the number of years of service and age. If the total was 85 you could retire, and now the window said one only needed 82. In addition to me, Mingus would lose two great teachers. Tom was a great math teacher who had done much for Mingus. Joan Evans was a business teacher who coached our FBLA (Future Business Leaders of America) to first place in the state over 20 straight years.

When I was in the Marine Corps, we had to fall out often for a ceremony honoring old Marines who were retiring after 30 years of devoted service. Once I remarked to my sergeant the retiree could now enjoy life a lot more. He replied, "He'll spend every day in a bar drinking with buddies and talking about old battles. He won't last a year."

Many people told me the same thing. One must keep busy to enjoy a longer life. I decided I would keep busy and avoid the temptation to just sit around doing nothing but watching TV and reading. Carroll was certainly for this since I wouldn't always be underfoot around the house.

I became an adjunct faculty teacher at our community college and joined reading and writing groups at the library. I became a charter member of the new Toastmaster club in Cottonwood and continued to bowl in several leagues. Carroll requested I should now go to Randall's Restaurant for breakfast every day so she wouldn't have to get up early to fix breakfast for me. (I couldn't even fry an egg), however, I continued to get up around 5 a.m. because I couldn't convince Socrates, our black lab, to reset his clock. He let me know he wasn't retiring. It had always been his job to get me up to start the coffee and read the paper.

I also belonged to an exercise group but often didn't have time to exercise in a regular program. Everything considered I began to enjoy my free unscheduled time. The only problem was looking at the high school. I felt some pangs of regret because I envied both the teachers and students who together would read and discuss great moments from history and literature. I also envied those teachers as they shared stories with each other about things that happened in their classrooms during the day. I missed the camaraderie most of all. I realized they were having a great adventure and building memories they could carry into their own retirement as I have. I hope teachers appreciate the fact they are having the time of their lives doing a job they love. I knew I did, and I was both sorry and glad when it came to an end.

A.L. Tennyson's poem, Ulysses sums up my feelings.

How dull it is to pause, to make an end
To rust unburnished, not to shine in use!
As tho to breathe were life . . .
Tho much is taken, much abides; and tho'

Ernie Gabrielson

> *We are not now that strength which in old days*
> *Moved earth and heaven. That which we are, we are—*
> *One equal temper of heroic heart.*
> *Made weak by time and fate, but strong in will*
> *To strive, to seek, to find, and not to yield.*